The hair on her arms rose.

This handsome stranger must be her sister's surly, grumpy neighbor, Ryder Frost. And that must be the vicious terror who was always coming into Cara's yard. Cara had expressly warned Chanel to stay away from them both.

Ryder held up a hand. "Easy now, Cara. I'm not about to engage in another shouting match with you because of Wolf." Hearing him call her by her sister's name gave Chanel a jolt. She stuck her tongue between her teeth to keep from correcting him.

"I'll be getting on my way. C'mon, boy. Let's go."

Wolf gave a growl and hunkered down on the doormat.

"I don't know what's gotten into him," Ryder said.

"Yes, you do," she accused, taking on Cara's attitude. "He does this all the time." Well, she hoped he did.

Ryder looked away. "I don't know what it is about your porch or yard that draws him over here. I've tried keeping him away."

"Yes, well, do more than try."

Zoey Marie Jackson loves writing sweet romances. She is almost never without a book and reads across genres. Originally from Jamaica, West Indies, she has earned degrees from New York University; State University of New York at Stony Brook; Teachers College, Columbia University; and Argosy University. She's been an educator for over twenty years. Zoey loves interacting with her readers. You can connect with her at zoeymariejackson.com.

Books by Zoey Marie Jackson

Love Inspired

The Adoption Surprise
The Christmas Switch

Visit the Author Profile page at LoveInspired.com.

The
Christmas Switch

Zoey Marie Jackson

LOVE INSPIRED
INSPIRATIONAL ROMANCE

LOVE INSPIRED®
INSPIRATIONAL ROMANCE

Recycling programs
for this product may
not exist in your area.

ISBN-13: 978-1-335-58534-9

The Christmas Switch

Copyright © 2022 by Michelle Z. Jackson

All rights reserved. No part of this book may be used or reproduced in
any manner whatsoever without written permission except in the case of
brief quotations embodied in critical articles and reviews.

This is a work of fiction. Names, characters, places and incidents are either the
product of the author's imagination or are used fictitiously. Any resemblance
to actual persons, living or dead, businesses, companies, events or locales is
entirely coincidental.

For questions and comments about the quality of this book, please contact us
at CustomerService@Harlequin.com.

Love Inspired
22 Adelaide St. West, 41st Floor
Toronto, Ontario M5H 4E3, Canada
www.LoveInspired.com

Printed in U.S.A.

And ye shall seek me, and find me,
when ye shall search for me with all your heart.
—*Jeremiah* 29:13

I would like to dedicate this book to my son Jordan, though I doubt he will ever read it, LOL. He is one of the strongest people I know. I must acknowledge my husband, John, a constant source of support who helps keep me grounded and who never hesitates to pray when I need it. Special mention to my son Eric, and Arielle, Erika, Erin, Dezirae, Devyn, Destinee and Siara.

Thank you to my sister, Sobi Burbano, and Fran Purnell: my unofficial first reads crew. Thank you to my critique partner and fellow author, Vanessa Miller. Thank you to my Sisters Group, who helped me get this word count in. Also, this story wouldn't be what it is without the superb efforts of the Harlequin team: Dina, Melissa and others. And a big thank-you to my wonderful agent, who has such a sweet spirit and bright smile, Latoya Smith.

Chapter One

Chanel Houston tossed her keys in her purse and reached into the back seat of her sister's 2002 Honda Civic to grab one of the boxes of books. She had packed a couple of medium boxes, intending to use her unexpected "vacation" to catch up on some reading.

She closed the door, already missing her Chevy Trailblazer, and made her way up the three rickety steps of the place she had spent a few summers as a teen. Brushing her hands across her gray hooded sweater and jean shorts, Chanel stood before the entrance of her grandparents' home—a nineteenth-century historical landmark boasting six bedrooms, three baths, a wrap-around porch, a vegetable garden and a small pond—and shook her head.

The things you do for your sister. Your identical twin sister.

Things like switching places when you're a grown woman. Her sister, Cara, a detective at the Hawk's Landing Police Department, was working with the FBI on a secret case and needed the people of her small hometown in Delaware to believe she was still here. So of course she had called her convenient stand-in to switch with her until Christmas. Chanel and Cara had met up in Sussex County to switch cars, clothes and keys. It was more than a coincidence that Chanel had just resigned from her job as a librarian in Newport News, Virginia.

She stopped at the top of the stairs and groaned. Oh no. She had thrown the key ring holding the house and car keys in her black hole of a purse… Placing the box on the ground, Chanel rummaged around in her bag for the keys.

While she searched, an odd sensation of being watched crawled up her spine. She turned but saw nothing in the dim lighting.

Scolding her overactive imagination, Chanel plopped the bag on the floor and stooped to conduct a more thorough search. Great. After a four-hour ride, she was sweaty and could use a drink of water.

She felt a small, wet imprint on the back of her leg. Followed by heavy breathing. Panting.

Her body tensed. That didn't sound like a deer.

Grabbing a travel-sized umbrella out of her bag, Chanel whipped around, her bottom landing hard on the wooden porch. She yelped and met the blue-eyed gaze of a Siberian husky, taking in his white fur and hanging tongue. Her eyes went wide.

He snarled, watching her but otherwise standing still.

Realizing he was a puppy and had no intentions of harming her, Chanel reached out to ruffle his right ear, her other hand actively feeling around in her bag for the keys.

"Hey, boy." She giggled and touched her chest. "You gave me quite a scare. Don't you know better than to creep up on people like that? Huh?"

The animal moved closer to rub his nose against

her arm before settling beside her. His shiny coat was soft. She could see the pup was well-groomed; someone was definitely missing their pet. She pushed her box of books into a corner and stretched her legs. Cocking her head, Chanel asked, "Where's your owner, big guy?"

A throat cleared. "He's right here."

Chantal lifted her head to meet another blue-eyed gaze. This one belonged to a lean man a couple inches over six feet, with ash-blond hair and keen eyes filled with skepticism and wariness. He was dressed in a green polo and tan khakis, and not a single strand of hair was out of place. For a split second, she lost her voice, which was fine because the stranger continued.

"Go ahead. Let me have it." He arched a brow, crossed his arms and waited.

Have what? Chanel racked her brain wondering who this might be. Cara hadn't described this handsome stranger when she'd mentioned who Chanel might encounter. If she had, Chanel would have remembered him. However, it was obvious this man expected her to know his identity, so she willed her tongue to move. The man held out a hand, an unspoken offer to help her get on her feet.

"I don't know what you expect me to say." She dusted off her shorts, particles making her cough. The dog closed his eyes as if bored with the conversation swirling around him. "I was just messing around with your dog." She struggled to get to her feet on her own before accepting his help.

His larger hands gripped hers. A faint electricity passed between them. Chanel broke contact as soon as she was steady.

His eyes narrowed. "I'm surprised to see you get close to Wolf. I'm even more surprised that you're capable of talking without yelling." He gave a chuckle filled with a mix of suspicion and humor.

At those words, the hair on her arms rose. Chanel knew who this was. This must be her sister's surly, grumpy neighbor, Ryder Frost, who had moved in six months ago. She looked at the pup sprawled on the floor. *And this must be the vicious terror who is always coming into Cara's yard.* Cara had expressly warned Chanel to stay away from them both. Menaces, she'd called them.

Chanel eyed the beautiful dog, who was staring at her with pleading eyes. She didn't know how she was going to resist their pull. Even now, her fingers itched to play in his glossy mane. Chanel was a dog lover, and trying to stay away would be torture. But somehow, she must. Cara had been bitten by dogs twice, and that had sealed her dislike for life. Because of that, Chanel had never owned one. But her first job had been in a pet store as a groomer in the next town, so she had been given many opportunities to play with other people's dogs.

She licked her dry lips, tugged on a tendril of her shoulder-length curls and then shot back. "Well, goes to show that you might not always know a person." Inside her chest, her heart raced. She hoped he bought her flippant response; otherwise her ruse might be up before it began. Like a tennis player, she waited for him to serve his comeback.

Ryder held up a hand. "Easy now, Cara. I'm not about to engage in another shouting match with you because of Wolf." Hearing him call her by her sister's name gave Chanel a jolt. She stuck her tongue between her teeth to keep from correcting him. And, oh, how she wanted to. Instead, she kept up her search for the keys.

"I'll be getting on my way." Ryder gave a shrill whistle. Wolf opened his eyes, then turned his head and closed them. Ryder's face reddened. He took a tentative step. "C'mon, boy. Let's go."

Wolf gave a growl and hunkered down on the front door mat.

"I don't know what's gotten into him," Ryder said.

"Yes, you do," she accused, taking on Cara's attitude. "He does this all the time." Well, she hoped he did. Her mind raced to recall. The only thing that truly registered in this moment was that she needed to suggest Cara check her vision. The man before her was not a beast.

Aha! Success. Her fingers curled around the keys.

Ryder looked away, his hair falling into his face. "I don't know what it is about your porch or yard that draws him over here. I've tried keeping him away."

"Yes, well. Do more than *try* and keep him away from my vegetable garden," Chanel said, remembering Cara's chief complaint. She opened the front door, knowing she had to get away from these two before she confessed. What she wanted to do was offer the dog some water or a snack. Chanel stepped behind the screen and into the house, then turned, intending to close the door.

Ryder bent over and scooped the dog into his arms, his muscles bulging. Chanel admired his strength. Ryder Frost was in great physical shape.

Then she saw a small figure approach. One that turned her legs into concrete.

"Daddy, I was looking for you," the little girl said in a booming voice with a slight lisp. She looked to be about five years old and wore a sunflower dress, white cardigan, white frilly socks and black Mary Janes. Her blond hair had been pulled into a neat bun, and she wore a headband with a sunflower. Then she pinned Chanel with eyes similar to Ryder's before lifting her head to ask her father, "Daddy, did Wolf get out again?"

She racked her brain to remember if Cara had mentioned her neighbor had a daughter. She touched her chest. The familiar ache returned for the child she would never have. All that had been buried along with her husband.

Ryder must have nodded, because Chanel heard her say, "Bad doggy. You need to stay over at our house." That earnest face was a shock to Chanel's system, bringing a hope she thought dead alive. The screen was a poor shield against the cute package mere feet away.

"We're sorry to bother you," Ryder said, turning to leave. He gestured toward the little girl. "Let's go, Gabby."

Her name was Gabby. Short for Gabrielle, maybe?

"Wait," Chanel breathed out and pointed to the dog. She found she wasn't ready for this family to leave. That was strange because she had lived on her own for years and hadn't had a problem being alone. Maybe it was coming back to this house. This place. The first question that jumped into her mind popped out. "What made you decide to call him Wolf?"

"I named him that," Gabby said in a loud voice, stepping close to the screen door. "Cause he's a cousin of the wolf family. Daddy got him for me."

Chanel felt her lips twitch, and she tried to keep up Cara's persona. Her mother had said there was no such thing as a stranger with Chanel. She made friends quick and easy, always ready for a conversation. Unlike Cara, who was more reserved and suspicious—traits well suited for her career. Cara wouldn't be smiling right now. She would go into inquisition mode. But at this moment, Chanel took over, did what she wanted to do. And what Chanel wanted to do was smile.

Her smile was electrifying. It evened out the sharp planes of her face and softened her look, making her countenance shine. Ryder Frost clamped his jaw shut and cuddled Wolf closer to his chest. He hadn't known Cara Shelton was capable of smiling, but he knew better than to say so. Cara always had a frown or smirk on her face when dealing with him. He took in her widened lips and white teeth, then dared to explore further.

Since he had moved to Hawk's Landing, he had never engaged in a good conversation with his neighbor. The fact that, as a white man, he had purchased a plot of land once belonging to slave-owners had been a sore point for Cara and others in town—but for Ryder, it was about the architecture.

And forget about his dog. Her lips curled every time she saw Wolf. The dog preferred her place to his: her porch, her yard, her vegetables.

Ryder had been in his kitchen, putting the finishing touches on his dinner—baked chicken breast with roasted brussels sprouts—when he realized Wolf wasn't in the house. Shoving the pans into the oven and setting a timer on his watch, Ryder had rushed across the lawn to Cara's yard, mentally preparing himself for another battle.

Yet here she was smiling, her beautiful white teeth on display.

His brows rose. Answered prayer? He had asked God on many occasions to give him patience when it came to Cara Shelton.

She flicked the switch to turn on both the inside and outside lights. Wolf jumped out of Ryder's arms, rubbing his body against the screen door, and Gabby moved to pet him. "Good dog. Good dog." Then she wagged her finger. "You need to listen to me and Daddy."

Since Cara was only a few inches shorter than he was, and in his line of sight, Ryder took in her beautiful brown skin, the light freckles dusting her nose and cheeks, her high cheekbones and honey-colored eyes surrounded by thick, long lashes. He acknowledged his neighbor's physical attractiveness. Every time he had seen her, she had her hair in a bun or ponytail. Today, she had it loose and flowing. Ryder liked it. However, for him it was all about a woman's substance and inner beauty. He cleared his throat. Not that he was interested in dating. He had his research and Gabby to fill his days. Ryder backed up. It was time for him to go home.

He opened his mouth to say his farewell when he saw Chanel watching Gabby with a tender expression. She placed a hand over her abdomen. In that unguarded moment, a sadness and yearning filled her eyes before she shuttered it with her lashes.

Without taking her gaze off Gabby and Wolf, she asked, "How old is she?"

"She's five," he said.

"Where's her mom?" she asked, then put a hand over her mouth. "I'm sorry. I didn't mean to pry."

Ryder shook his head. "It's all right," he said, dabbing at his brow and ignoring the rumble of his stomach. He needed to eat, but his stomach could wait while he discovered what it was like to exchange pleasantries with his neighbor.

"Naw. I need to learn to mind my business," she said, flailing a hand. "Forget I asked. My mother always told me that my mouth was not my own."

The screen door creaked, and she returned outside to

slink into one of the wooden rocking chairs. Gabby and Wolf ran down the steps to frolic in the high grass. It needed to be cut. It had been raining a lot over the past several days, causing more growth. Ryder had passed over his lawn with the riding mower early that morning and was tempted to do the same for Cara. But he'd refrained, not sure if his good deed would be welcomed or appreciated.

Gabby began doing backflips while Wolf ran beside her. Ryder walked over to the other rocking chair and sat. He and Cara sat watching Gabby's and Wolf's antics for a few minutes before he decided to answer Cara's question. He felt comfortable sharing because, as his neighbor, she would have noted he was alone when he'd first moved next door in May.

"Four months ago, my doorbell rang, and I opened the door to see the sister of an old colleague, a fellow researcher." He jutted his chin toward Gabby. "Her mother. With her." Then he coughed, feeling a tickle in his throat.

"Do you want something to drink?" Cara asked, jumping to her feet.

His eyes went wide. "Yeah, uh, sure." He coughed again, placing his hand over his mouth.

"Hang on," she said. "I'll be back."

Ryder twisted his body to watch her bounce through the door, and he scrunched his nose. It felt like he was talking to a completely different person, because Cara was being so—well, neighborly. He laughed at his paranoia and shook his head.

A couple minutes later, Cara returned, carrying a tray. "I could use a little help here," she said in singsong voice.

Ryder held the screen door open, battling a feeling

of surrealness. Cara had placed two tall glasses and a smaller glass of lemonade and an old bowl filled with water on the tray. He was taken aback at her thoughtfulness in including Wolf. He thanked her for the drink and watched as she served his daughter and dog.

"Say thank you to Ms. Cara," Ryder prompted.

"Thank you," Gabby said, sitting on the top step with Wolf lapping away next to her.

After taking a few sips, Gabby returned to play, taking advantage of the little sunlight that was left. Fanning herself, Cara returned to the rocking chair. It creaked with her movements.

"So, I take it her mother left her with you?" she asked, laying her head back.

"Yes, Brittany—that's her mother's name—had an opportunity to go to Egypt to study the pyramids and decided it was time I met my daughter. She told me it would be for a few weeks, but as you see, it has turned into months. Not that I mind." He spoke those words with wry humor, although he had had a different reaction that day. He'd been sucker punched. Speechless. And scared.

Cara leaned forward, her mouth dropping open. "This is better than any novel I've ever read. You had a secret love child?"

He patted his brow. "I don't know if I would call what we had...*love*. Before I accepted God in my life, Brittany and I had a brief...encounter. She had accompanied my coworker to a convention we were both attending. We spent hours talking about my research and her studies in Egyptology. After that one weekend, we parted ways."

She chuckled, then said in a dry tone, "The encounter might have been brief, but the repercussions are lasting."

"Yes. Well." Ryder gave a dismissive wave to cover his embarrassment. "In the four months Gabby has been here, I can honestly say I have no regrets. But I didn't know anything about children. I was an only child of parents who were also only children. YouTube is a divine gift. It has saved me on many occasions. It's my go-to for everything from combing her hair to coordinating her clothes. Being a parent is more challenging than my first dissertation."

"But I'm sure it's rewarding." She gazed at Gabby, her eyes bright. "From what I see, she seems happy, so you must be doing something right." This time, there was no mistaking the yearning in her tone. She smirked. "Although I reserve the right to be wrong. Just giving my first—um, my *overall* impression."

"I'm glad I didn't mess up," he said, not quite sure what to do about the fact that his neighbor was giving him a compliment instead of her usual criticism.

"Some of us would have loved the chance…to mess up," Cara said before lowering her lashes and sipping her lemonade.

Ryder scooted forward, searching for the courage to ask if she had children. He hadn't seen any, but the papers said she had been a cop for close to 14 years. Cara was probably in early forties and could have grown children in college. Just as he opened his mouth, his timer went off.

Chapter Two

She'd wanted to say yes. Yes to having dinner with Ryder, to joining him and Gabby for chicken and brussels sprouts when he had extended the invitation. Her tummy appreciated anyone with culinary skills. But she'd declined his offer, knowing Cara wouldn't have accepted, and had eaten a couple of frozen waffles instead before spending the rest of the evening cleaning and dusting.

Chanel wasn't much of a cook, which was why she was now heading toward the town square at six o'clock the next morning to purchase muffins. Though she had fallen asleep after midnight the night before after speaking with Cara, Chanel was an early riser. She didn't like sleeping long. Sleeping meant dreaming. Dreaming about Warren's death.

It was early November, and that meant Mrs. Collins would have pumpkin-spice muffins. Her mouth watered and her stomach growled in anticipation when she pictured the decadent display inside the huge glass.

Today, the temperature had dropped a few degrees, which was great for fall weather, so she had donned a mauve Guess tracksuit with a pair of New Balances be-

fore driving a quarter mile to Collins' Grocer & Bakery.
Cara's cupboards and refrigerator were empty. Like her
sister, Chanel ate a lot of fruits and veggies, but she also
had a sweet tooth. There wasn't a doughnut, Ho Ho or
MoonPie safe from meeting her lips. Fortunately, they
hadn't found their way to her hips since she ran or cy-
cled so she could eat what she wanted.

Chanel drove past the cornfields and chicken farms
until she reached a fork in the road. The left would lead
to the town's sole strip mall, movie theater and grocery
store. She swerved right, going past three large houses
before turning down the gravel path of the circular entrance and pulling into the parking lot next to a burgundy pickup truck.

The other vehicle in the lot was a lime-green 1966
Chevy Impala, which belonged to Mrs. Collins. The
shop owner had driven that same car when Chanel and
Cara came to visit in their youth. She used to give them
joyrides, speeding on the back roads, with Cara and
Chanel laughing and screaming at the top of their lungs.

Chanel checked her purse to make sure she had
enough cash to pay for her goods and then exited her
car, careful to avoid stepping in a huge puddle. It had
rained for close to an hour the night before, but it should
be sunny for most of the day.

Opening the door to the store, she smiled at the
clamoring ring of the bell and the sound of Christmas
music—yes, Christmas music. Chanel sniffed, welcoming the aroma of cinnamon and pumpkin spice. She
licked her lips, thinking about the warm glaze drizzling
down the sides of the muffin, and grabbed a small black
shopping cart. One of the rickety wheels cling-clanged,
but Chanel didn't swap out. If memory served, every
single cart had something wrong—or, as Mrs. Collins

said, something *unique*. Mrs. Collins hated throwing anything out, as was evident by all the sixties, seventies and eighties paraphernalia sprinkled throughout the store. Portraits, license plates and other knickknacks had been glued or nailed to the wooden ceiling, which the older woman said gave her store character.

She ducked past the beaded curtain placed above the first aisle and spotted the store owner unpacking a box of pumpkin cans. She waved at Mrs. Collins, who beckoned her over.

"How's it going?" the older woman asked. She was dressed in a pair of baggy jeans and a colorful shirt along with her ever-present store apron. "That was some nasty business with Jeremiah Greene."

Cara had told her all about the man who had killed three high school students and who had escaped on her sister's watch. It had been a long time since Chanel had heard her sister cry for hours. She had vowed to find him, which was why Cara had pretended to quit her job at the station and gone undercover, sending Chanel here to secretly take her place.

Picking up some cans and placing them on the shelf, Chanel assumed her sister's demeanor. Mrs. Collins knew everyone, so it was important that she convince the other woman that she was her sister.

Lowering her head, she pictured Cara's heartbroken face to guide her taut emotions. "You don't know how that haunts me. That I failed." Chanel's voice hitched. She felt her sister's pain like it was her own. Blinking back tears, she continued to stack the cans and compose herself. Her sister would be emotional, but she wouldn't fall apart. She had too much strength for that.

Mrs. Collins placed a wrinkled, brown, spotted hand on Chanel's arm. "Oh, dearie. Nobody blames you. You stopped to help someone else in need. Wasn't no need for you to up and quit like that."

Chanel faced the other woman, whose eyes reflected warmth and compassion. "I couldn't continue working. I can't look those family members in their eyes," she whispered.

Mrs. Collins nodded. "I understand. Stop punishing yourself." She tilted her head. "You're too young to just sit home. What you plan on doing with yourself?"

"I haven't figured it out yet."

The front door chimed, which distracted Mrs. Collins long enough for Chanel to escape and finish her shopping.

Going to the back of the store, she picked up a quart of milk to have with her muffins. Next, she went to the fresh-goods section and snagged a bag of peaches and then a carton of strawberries that were on sale and featured on a checkered tablecloth. Eyeing the bananas on another table, Chanel fought to turn the cart, but the wheel got stuck on the tablecloth. Bending over, she yanked on the material wedged in the wheel until she heard a deep voice. One she already recognized.

"Need some help?" Ryder asked, parking his cart across from hers.

"Yes, please," she said before clamping her tongue between her teeth. Her messy bun had already begun coming loose because of her efforts.

He crouched close and grabbed the edge of the cloth while she lifted the wheel. Chanel caught a whiff of sandalwood, nutmeg and mandarin—a pleasing woodsy smell. He was dressed in a long-sleeved black polo and a pair of black slacks. The dark color was a nice contrast against skin the color of sand.

It took a couple of trials, but they managed to free

her cart. Chanel stood and grabbed the handle. "Thank you. I don't know how I managed to do that," she said, putting space between them. She turned to continue her shopping.

"I'm glad I was able to help," he said, stepping beside her. The aisle was more suited for one person, so their carts bumped. His had eggs, cheese, milk, green peppers, turkey bacon and other items that made her think of omelets, how much she loved them and how jealous she was because she wasn't going to be having any.

Chanel stopped walking and picked up a can of beans, hoping he would be on his way. Otherwise, she would be tempted to chitchat. If there was a longer way to say something, Chanel would use it. Her sister was the one with few words. Chanel loved words.

Apparently, Ryder did also. "What brings you here?" he asked, in a tone way too chipper for the hour.

"Where's Gabby?" she asked instead of answering his question.

"She's in the bakery section, bending Mrs. Collins's ear." He chuckled. "Gabby spotted the apple fritters and made a beeline for them."

Chanel bit back a smile. Gabby had good taste. She would need to add fritters to her list. Hunching her shoulders, she said, "Well, I'd better get going. I've got a lot to do." She pushed off.

"Sure. See you around, neighbor." Ryder gave a small wave, his brows furrowed.

She swallowed her guilt over seeing the confusion in Ryder's eyes, like he was wondering what he had done to ruin their rapport from the previous day. She couldn't tell him that he had done nothing wrong and that talking to him felt very right. She wasn't ready to wonder why.

Chanel headed to the bathroom to hide out until

Ryder and Gabby departed. Once they were gone, she'd grab her baked goods and take a different route home to ensure she would get back after them. Chanel exhaled. Avoiding the man next door would not be easy.

Ryder finished his shopping and thanked Mrs. Collins for entertaining Gabby while he gathered the rest of his items. The older woman was a huge help. Before Gabby, Ryder had never engaged in small talk, but the first time he had ventured inside with her had ended with apples all over the store. Since then, Mrs. Collins kept Gabby occupied, giving him a chance to move through the aisles without incident.

That morning, Ryder had awakened in the mood for omelets and breakfast potatoes, so once he had gotten himself and Gabby dressed, he rushed over to the grocer's. Ryder liked to make Gabby a large breakfast every day and pack her lunch from home. When she first came to live with him, Gabby had climbed onto the cupboard to get a bowl to make herself some cereal. That had melted his heart. It was obvious his daughter was used to tending to her own needs. He wasn't surprised because, like Brittany, he could get caught up in his research and forget to eat until he was done.

However, since Gabby's arrival, he had changed his behavior patterns. Taking care of her gave him an internal sense of joy and satisfaction, filling a need he'd had no idea existed. Family.

Just as they got close to the vehicle, Gabby twisted out of his grip and jumped into a huge puddle.

"Why did you do that?" he scolded. "Now your shoes are filled with mud."

Gabby shrugged. "I don't know."

"Stay here," he directed, holding her shoulders until she stood still.

Ryder swallowed his annoyance and moved his eyes away from that cute little face. She was being a kid, and kids jumped into puddles. What he should have done was warn her not to do so. One day he would get the hang of this parenting thing.

He blew out a huge plume of air, opened his truck and dropped his groceries on the passenger seat. Then he hoisted Gabby into his arms.

"Wheee," she said, swaying her body.

Ryder was about to put her in her car seat when he noticed her small hand gripped a huge chocolate chip cookie, which he had agreed she could have with her lunch at school. Some of the chocolate chips had melted along her palms and fingers. Ryder had learned to keep the wipes handy because they cleaned everything—spills, chocolate, markers. Wipes and Ziploc bags were his two must-haves.

He went around his truck to get baby wipes out of the glove box and wiped Gabby's hands, shoes and leggings.

As he cleaned, he thought about his wishy-washy neighbor. When he'd seen Cara struggling with the cart, he'd been eager to assist and continue their conversation. A loner by nature, Ryder wasn't sure why his tongue had loosened around her yesterday or why his heart rate seemed to quicken in her presence. That had never happened before, but he liked her sense of humor. Especially since he hadn't known Cara even possessed one.

However, today, she had been...standoffish.

He grabbed a Ziploc bag and dropped Gabby's cookie inside before placing it on the front passenger seat.

"I want my cookie," Gabby whined.

"You can have it with lunch," he reminded her.

Ryder found himself dragging out the task of settling Gabby into her car seat, looking behind him to see if Chanel would come out of the store. After a few minutes, he glanced at his watch and knew he couldn't lag or Gabby would have to eat breakfast at school. Ryder backed out of the lane, keeping his eye trained on the front door, but Cara remained inside.

"Daddy, I don't want green peppers in my om-ah-let," Gabby said, her loud voice echoing in the small space.

"Okay, I won't put any in your *omelet*," he said, correcting her pronunciation before peering into the rearview mirror to glance at his child. She was dressed in a long-sleeved shirt with a doughnut on her chest and leggings that featured tiny replicas of the doughnut. Ryder had purchased the outfit from Amazon, and he had another package due from Walmart soon. Gabby had grown about three inches and needed a new wardrobe and shoes for her rabbit-like feet.

A few minutes later, he turned down the gravel path to his driveway. This time, Ryder made sure to warn his daughter to avoid the muddy puddles. While she changed into another outfit, he worked on the omelets and breakfast potatoes. Though Ryder liked historic homes, he appreciated modern luxuries, so he had gutted the interior of the kitchen and installed stainless steel appliances and marble countertops in the open space, knowing he would spend a lot of time there.

Growing up in foster homes, Ryder had dreamed of sitting around a breakfast table with people who cared about him, who didn't see him as a detriment to their income or a nuisance. The kitchen was the heart of the home. That's why he had a round white table and chairs in the center along with a nook with sofa cushions. His heart had warmed the first time Gabby had curled into the corner with a book on her lap, reading while he cooked.

Gabby returned, wearing jeans and a long-sleeved shirt with a ballerina on her chest. When she sat at the table, Ryder said grace, served Gabby a small portion of food and added a dollop of ketchup to her plate before placing a disposable white plastic bib around her neck. There would be no more outfit changes.

Once they had blessed their meal, they dug in. After the first bite, Ryder nodded with satisfaction. Gabby smacked her lips. Everything was just right.

A few minutes later, Gabby placed the last potato in her mouth and wiped her face with the back of her hand. "Can we give some to Wolf?"

Wolf.

Ryder paused before scrunching his nose. He didn't remember seeing Wolf when he'd entered. He cocked his head. His mind had been centered on getting breakfast ready and Gabby re-dressed for school.

Oh, no. If Wolf wasn't here, it meant he had escaped through the doggy door in the kitchen. Ryder must have forgotten to close it before leaving. Again.

Ryder's chair scraped across the wooden floor as he bounded to his feet, then slipped into his boots. He yanked open the door and scanned Cara's yard. Seeing the bus pull up, he yelled out to Gabby to grab her lunch bag and her backpack. Then he scooped her under his arm and dashed down the driveway before the bus could pull off. Mr. Atkins had a ten-second-wait rule. She giggled, probably enjoying how her body flopped like a puppet the entire way.

After shaking his head, Ryder kissed her cheeks. "Have a good day."

"See you later," she said before making her way up the steps.

Ryder always felt a pang watching her get onto the bus. He looked to Mr. Atkins for commiseration, but the older man pursed his lips and closed the door.

Remembering Wolf, Ryder slapped his forehead and ran into Cara's yard. By this time, the sun was out, drying up the damp earth. Though the grass was high, Ryder could see Wolf's white fur covered in mud. His paws were busy digging holes in Cara's vegetable garden.

"Wolf! Stop!" he called out.

The dog just kept digging. Ryder drew close, noticing the carrots tossed around the yard. Some were chewed. Some were smashed. None seemed salvageable. "Get home," he commanded.

Ryder lunged, but Wolf took off, running back onto Ryder's property. He heard a door slam behind him and turned to face Cara with dread. To his surprise, she was laughing—she was pointing her finger, doubled over and laughing at him.

He looked down and gasped. He had stepped in a huge pile of poop. Wolf's parting gift. As Ryder lifted his leg, the scent hit his nostrils, and he gagged. "Ugh. Wolf knows better than to do this."

She snorted. A very unladylike snort. "I know I should be mad, but this is hilarious. You should have gotten a cat, and your dog needs training." She pulled out her phone and snapped a picture of him. Then another.

"The only pet store in town closed, so I have to train him myself. I've watched several YouTube videos, but they aren't much help." Hearing another snap, he pointed. "Delete those pics. I wouldn't have stepped in poo if your grass wasn't so high."

"You wouldn't have stepped in it if your dog was in his own yard," she shot back.

Ryder made a move toward her just as she took another photograph. He knew his face was beet red, but he hated how she was having fun at his mortification.

"No way." Shaking her head, she started backing up. Slipping her phone into her back pocket, she said, "Don't move." Her laughter escalated like musical keys on a scale until tears rolled down her cheeks. "This is the best thing I've seen all morning." She dashed to the side of the house.

A few seconds later, he heard the unmistakable sound of the hose. Before Ryder could protest, Cara turned the water on him full force, washing away the grime from his legs and boots. He clamped his jaw shut, fully intending to toss his outfit in the garbage. This humiliation wouldn't be easy to erase from his mind anytime soon. His only minor consolation was that she was also getting wet in the process.

"Turn it off now, please," he yelled once his boots were clean. "I'm glad the sun is out or I would be worried about catching a cold."

She complied and returned the hose to its base.

"I'm sorry about all this." He swept his hand across the yard. "I'll repair your vegetable garden."

"You don't have to. I can do it," she said, waving a hand.

"I insist. I can help you or hire a handyman." He gave Cara his cell number and watched her long fingers put his contact information into her phone. "Text me so I know it's you. I don't answer the phone unless I know who's calling or texting. Too many spam callers."

"Yes, I can't stand the random robocalls. People have nothing better to do with their time." She placed a hand on her hip. "If you want, I could train your dog. I worked at a pet store in my teens, and that was one of my responsibilities."

All Ryder could do was nod. "This has been a most… humbling experience." Without making eye contact, he turned toward his house with the peanut-sized pride he had left.

He heard a chuckle behind him.

"I think the word you're looking for is *unforgettable*," she said.

Chapter Three

"Why didn't you capture it on video?" Cara asked Chanel on FaceTime that night. "That would have been epic." Her sister's eyes were filled with mirth at her neighbor's debacle. Because of that, Cara wasn't as mad about Wolf destroying her vegetables, stating she wouldn't be there to eat them anyway—if there were any left after the rabbits got to them. Chanel didn't mention Gabby, and Cara didn't either.

"I took a couple of pictures, but there's no way I'm sending them to you."

"You're no fun," Cara joked.

"Really? You're saying that when I agreed to switch places with you?" Chanel shifted on the living room sofa and slapped her leg. "Did you forget all the fun we used to have fooling people?"

"Nope. Mom and Dad used to get furious with us."

Thinking of her deceased parents made Chanel sadden. "I miss them."

"I do too. They were the best…" Their parents had died within months of each other. Her mother of a sudden stroke and her dad of a broken heart not too long after. He hadn't wanted to carry on without their mom.

A testimony of the close bond they had shared. Like the one Chanel shared with her sister.

Cara interrupted her thoughts and shifted the conversation with a random observation. "Besides our parent, the only person who could tell us apart was Ms. Mavis."

Hearing the former librarian's name made Chanel's eyes go wide. "What if I run into her? Our cover could be blown." She fretted with her lip. "The entire town knows we're twins, so what's to stop somebody from casually bringing that up in conversation?" Her eyes went wide. "Does Ryder know you're a twin?"

Cara waved a hand. "No, why would I tell him? He doesn't need to know. In fact, he's a hermit and sticks to himself. And as for the town, it's been fifteen years since you left. You might not have lived there full-time for long, but having you gone was painful for all of us. Hardly anyone mentions you for that reason. Besides, a lot of people who knew us are retired and moved somewhere warmer or are six feet under. There's a lot of new people in town. I think you'll be fine."

She raised a brow at her sister's words. "Six feet under? Can't you come up with a more sympathetic phrasing?"

Cara shrugged, bringing Chanel's attention to her slim shoulders. Her face appeared gaunt, like she hadn't been sleeping. Chanel cocked her head. "How are you doing?"

Cara's expression closed. When it came to her job, she could be tight-lipped. Even now, she spoke to Chanel with the background blurred. This was for both their protection, but it made Chanel acutely aware of how dangerous this assignment was. "I'm managing."

Worry swirled like a building tornado, but Chanel knew better than to voice her fears. It would only put her sister on edge, and she needed Cara safe. Before Chanel had agreed to be Cara's stand-in, her twin told her that Jeremiah was a computer genius who had infiltrated the police station's intricate computer systems, so she needed to work with the FBI.

Cara had insisted on going deep undercover and being part of their investigation while they tracked Jeremiah's movements. Since Jeremiah had family in town who were covering for him and informing him, Cara had asked Chanel to do the switch. That was all her boss had allowed her to share. Chanel didn't know how her sister was able to put her life in danger like this, but Cara excelled at her job as a detective in Hawk's Landing.

Typical of Cara, she directed the conversation away from herself. "I should be home by Christmas, as promised. Can you stay until then?"

"Yes. Thanks to working nonstop, I had a good payout when I quit. They paid me all my sick leave and vacation days."

"Has your boss called to say they made a mistake?"

"Nope. They feel as if they made the right decision giving the promotion to Alma, though they asked if I could train her before leaving."

Chanel couldn't keep the bitterness out of her tone. Alma Tate was a younger Caucasian woman with a master's degree in fine arts. She had limited experience on how to run a library, but they had still chosen her over Chanel, who had years of experience, though her bachelor's degree was in agricultural studies. So Chanel had quit.

"I'm glad you left."

Clearing her throat, Chanel brought up another topic.

"Do you think it would be a red flag if I put up Christmas decorations?"

"Can we get through Thanksgiving first?" Cara scoffed.

"Quit being a grinch, and answer my question."

Her sister pondered for a beat and then shrugged. "Go ahead. Ryder is my only neighbor, and he has no idea what I do for the holidays. So I don't think it'd be a problem. Besides, if anyone from town ventured that far, they would think I'm doing it because I'm bored since I left the police force." Cara leaned closer, her tone changing when she spoke again. "How have you been sleeping?"

Chanel shifted, folding her legs under her. "I'm fine during the day. I feel like the prodigal son—or in this case, daughter—who returned home, and this house, the land, has welcomed me. We had so many great memories here as children. But at night, I'm in a mental tug-of-war between peace and panic. All I do is think of him."

Warren Houston. Her high school sweetheart and husband. He'd loved life. Even now, she could picture him—tall, powerful, strong.

Until he wasn't.

Because of her.

She sniffled.

"Warren wouldn't have wanted you to blame yourself like you've done for the past fifteen years," her sister said, eyes soft and tender. "He would have wanted you to grab your second chance and run with it."

"I didn't deserve to live," she whispered, tears seeping from the corners of her eyes.

"God must have thought so, or you wouldn't be here," Cara said, pleading. "He has plans for you. You can't be a Jonah forever. At some point, you have to be where He wants you to be, which is here in Hawk's Landing. It's home. I firmly believe that. That's why I wouldn't—*haven't*—sold that place. I've been waiting for you. When we were teenagers, we vowed to bring the farm back to its former glory, and that's what I intend to do. With you."

Her sister's chest rose and fell with each breath while she waited for Chanel to respond. Cara was right about her being home. That much she could agree with.

The rest, not so much.

The years melted as fresh pain bubbled into her chest, and words traveled from her heart to her lips. "He died trying to save me." Chanel's body shook under the weight of her guilt. "If I hadn't made Warren take the boat out for us to go fishing, he would be alive. And I wouldn't have lost—" She flung her head back and cried, her shoulders shaking, unable to bear the brunt of her sorrow. Her ache. Like a constant toothache, it gnawed at her, keeping her awake—in limbo, restless, paused in time.

Chanel sniffled. Her tear ducts were putting in overtime. The grief threatened to engulf her.

She heard her sister's gentle voice. "Get the box of tissue, and wipe your face." Once Chanel had done so, Cara asked her to meet her eyes. "You're the strongest person I know, but guilt will bury you deeper than quicksand. You don't control the weather. You couldn't have seen that storm coming. No one did. Not even the weatherman."

Chanel shuddered as she remembered that moment, when the boat capsized and the sail pierced her abdomen, causing her to lose their unborn baby.

Cara kept talking. "I smile when I think of Warren because he was your hero. He saved you, and if he had to decide, he would do it again. I have no doubt about that."

Chanel nodded, knowing Cara was right. "I can't do this farm without him. That wasn't the plan."

"You can and you must, or you will never be at peace. Fifteen years is a long time to carry the guilt like a hiker's backpack. You have to let it go. Cast your cares on Him. God said that for a reason." Her sister spoke with such certainty that Chanel felt the words take root within her.

"I'll pray on it." She licked her lips and then whispered her current biggest concern. "Ryder has a daughter. A little girl. Why didn't you tell me?"

"You know why, honey," Cara said. "If I had, you wouldn't have come."

"And you expect me to stay away from him?" Her chest tightened. "From her?"

Cara's eyes held empathy and understanding. "I see now that request was impossible. Unreasonable." She looked upward and chewed on her bottom lip, her eyes blinking rapidly while she processed.

She shrugged. "I don't think befriending them would appear out of character or do any harm. My disliking him and his dog has nothing to do with the case. But I think you do—like him, that is. Just act like me when you're around him." Cara waved at the screen. "Get rid of our pictures in the house in case he ever comes inside. And wear black. Dark colors, like I would."

Chanel laughed and tugged on the tracksuit she was wearing. "This was a gift I bought for you that you never wore."

A distraction in the background made Cara turn off her video and mute her microphone. Chanel's stomach muscles clenched, and she kept her eyes pinned to the screen. Several tense seconds passed before her sister returned. She could see Cara looked shaken, but she knew asking her to share would be pointless. All her sister said was she would be off the grid for a while and that she might not be able to call as much. With a nod, Chanel squelched her worry, uttered a quick prayer and begged her sister to stay safe.

Once she was off the call, Cara's words about her liking Ryder came back to her, and she frowned. Though Cara was cool with her chatting it up with her neighbor, Chanel didn't feel at ease now. Images of her and Ryder talking and laughing on the front porch, her hosing him down in the backyard filled her mind. It was all a bit too…close. Too companionable. Too…soon.

Chanel was friendly, but she wasn't sure she was ready for friendship with someone she found attractive. And the fact that each encounter with Ryder felt natural—easy—scared her. It had been easy with Warren, and look how that had ended.

Her cell pinged with a notification. When she saw Ryder's name, her heart rate accelerated. She swiped the screen to read the text message. When will you begin dog training and how much is your fee?

She read his words several times, analyzing them, contemplating how to respond. She wanted to keep her distance, but she had promised to train his dog. Chanel wanted to keep her word…

Maybe she could help with Wolf without having Ryder or Gabby around.

Chanel figured she would take a few days to get settled and get her mind in gear. The next time she saw Ryder, she would have her sister's mannerisms conquered. She glanced at her watch. It was close to eight o'clock. Not too late to respond. You don't have to pay me. Your dog will need a lot of training…

She hit the back button and deleted those words. She needed to be brief and not her usual long-winded self. She would just answer the question. Keep it simple. I'll start next week. No fee.

That was her impersonal, but necessary, response.

Ryder returned a couple of emails to his colleagues at the Sloan Kettering Institute, where he worked as a cancer geneticist. His focus was to study stem cell growth and tumor progression. Though he'd been on family leave since Brittany had dropped off Gabby on his doorstep, his colleagues often reached out to ask questions or run ideas by him because they knew he was a genius at what he did. They were feeling it with him not being there.

But he wasn't sure about going back full-time. At forty-three, he had years to go before retirement, but Ryder had worked at the institute for close to twenty years. All this time off with Gabby had him thinking about a career change, tackling something new. Like maybe teaching online. Although he loved what he did now, so he would have to think about it before making a decision.

Since the weather would be close to seventy degrees without any chance of rain, Ryder decided to cut his lawn. He went into the house to change into his old jeans, a faded shirt and the grass-stained black boots he wore when doing yardwork. He grabbed his Beats headphones and searched for TobyMac to pull up one of his albums. For once, Wolf remained at home, lying on the back porch, taking a nap.

He sauntered over to the shed and opened the door

to start up the John Deere Zero-Turn Mower he had purchased that summer. Navigating his way onto the grass, Ryder got lost in the worship music, whistling or belting out some of the lyrics. He finished his yard in about forty-five minutes. After catching sight of the thick patch on Cara's property, Ryder headed over to tackle her lawn, praying his prickly neighbor wouldn't accuse him of trespassing.

Thinking about Cara made his brows furrow. He hadn't been in a lot of relationships—partly because of his studies but also because Ryder had no intention of opening his heart to anyone. Not when his own parents had abandoned him, leaving him to the will of the state. It was better to be alone, depending on God and himself.

But he was drawn to Cara's optimism and her wit. Yet she confused him. Cara was like a water faucet running hot and cold. Take her text message response the night before: It was stiff. Formal. The complete opposite of the woman he was getting to know but characteristic of the one he had known all along. Which was the real Cara?

Turning up the volume when TobyMac's song "It's You" began to play, Ryder made his way around the perimeter of her yard. He would keep circling until he had completed the entire area.

Ryder lapped the huge circumference three times before he saw Cara waving at him from the back porch. She sat by a small glass table with two chairs, next to an oversize hammock that was in serious need of repair. Wolf was now stretched out by her feet like he lived there. Ryder shook his head. That dog. He used the back of his hand to wipe his brow and put the mower in park before waving back.

"You didn't have to do this," she yelled, gesturing for him to join her.

He held up a hand before turning off the motor, climbing down and walking over to where she sat. She was wearing a floral maxi dress and a straw hat. She held Christmas garlands in her hands and had a huge smile on her face.

Like he'd thought earlier, he didn't know how to read her these last few days. At least before, she had been constant in her loathing, and he'd known to keep his distance. Now she was a seesaw, and it made his head hurt. That didn't stop him from returning her smile or hurrying his steps, though. In fact, if he were being honest, his heart felt light.

Wolf opened one eye before closing it. Ryder smirked. His dog seemed quite content to pretend he didn't know Ryder. He'd remind Wolf of that when he came looking for food.

Ryder's eyes were drawn to the huge glass of water on the table with condensation running down the sides. His throat was dry. There was a platter with a couple of large muffins as well. His stomach growled at the sight.

"Thanks so much for taming our wildebeest of a lawn," she said, her voice bright and cheery as she rested the garlands across a chair. "I brought you some muffins and water because the sun is no joke and our—I mean, *my* yard is massive. I'm sure you must need hydration."

That was odd. Had she said *our* wildebeest of a lawn? To his knowledge, Cara lived alone. An ex-husband, maybe? Ryder was curious about the slip but decided not to question his neighbor—not when she was being sweet and thoughtful. He didn't want to be the thorn in her rosy demeanor.

"I could use some liquid hydration. Thanks." Ryder reached for the water and took several gulps. He hadn't realized how thirsty he was. He emptied the glass. "It's not a problem. My lawn mower is doing most of the work anyways."

"Still, I'm grateful because I wasn't looking forward to pushing that old mower out of the shed." She bit into a muffin. Some of the icing ended up on the sides of her mouth, reminding Ryder of his own hunger. He snatched one of the muffins, slipped into the chair across from her and took a huge bite. It was soft and moist and simply delicious. He slid a glance toward the plate; he might have to have another one.

"What were you listening to?" she asked. "I've been trying to get your attention for a while."

"TobyMac. Do you know him?"

"Yes," she said, gyrating her body. "I love him. Have you listened to his album called The Elements? 'It's You' is my jam."

His brows rose and he felt his eyes go wide. "I was literally just listening to that. It's one of my favorites on the entire album."

Their eyes held. It seemed like they meshed, had so much in common. There was a light breeze, causing her hair to frolic in the wind just so. He found it…appealing. He cleared his throat to break the spell and reached for another muffin. He figured if he were moving his mouth, he wouldn't do anything foolish, like tell her what he was thinking.

"I take it Gabby's in school?" Cara asked, looking out toward the yard.

"Yes. Although getting her on the bus this morning wasn't easy." He groaned. "She has a loose tooth and wanted to talk with her mom."

Cara watched him, a brow arched, curiosity in her eyes. "By your demeanor, I take it you couldn't reach her?"

"I tried, but the call went straight to voice mail. I didn't know what to think or what to say to Gabby. I hated to see her chin quiver and her eyes fill with tears. Nothing I said made her feel better. She didn't even look back at me when she got on the bus." His shoulders slumped. "She goes to school half-days, so I'll try again later. I pray that Brittany answers."

"Sometimes a girl just needs her mother," Cara said in a wistful tone.

He cocked his head and asked the question burning in his mind. "Do you have children?"

"No," she said, drumming her fingers on the table. "I can't anymore." Now *her* chin wobbled, and her eyes appeared slick.

Great. A second person crying today because of him. Ryder ran his hands through his hair. "I'm sorry. I shouldn't have pried."

"It's all right," she said softly before wiping her face. "I was pregnant once. With a girl." She met his eyes. Her next words stunned him into silence. "She would have been fifteen today if my careless actions…" She appeared to struggle for words before taking a deep breath and squaring her shoulders. "I lost her, and it was all my fault."

Somehow he doubted that. "What do you mean?" he asked gently.

"Can we not talk about this anymore? I've already said more than I meant to say, and losing a child the same day you lose your husband isn't easy…"

The relaxed banter between them dried like a raisin in the sun. Breaking eye contact, she had the look of someone ready to flee, but he wasn't ready for her to go.

"Sure. Uh, it wasn't my intention to… I'm sorry."

She gave a nod and stood. The chair made a scraping sound, jolting Wolf awake. "Let me put these decorations up."

Wolf chose that moment to provide a much-needed interruption. He bit into the garland, growling and gnawing on the snaky green invader, which made a light swishing sound on the porch when he shook it back and forth.

Cara bent down to pet his ears and gave a wobbly laugh. "Easy, boy. Let me have it." Once she had rescued the garland, she proceeded to wrap it around the banister. Sensing her discomfort, Ryder didn't tease her for putting out decorations so early. After she'd finished wrapping the garland, Chanel went in the house and returned with a fake snowman, which she placed a couple of feet from the door.

Wolf barked at it so much that Ryder decided to head home. He said his goodbyes, and Cara replied with, "I'll see you soon," while her tone said, *It doesn't matter if I do.*

Stuffing his hands into his pockets after Cara went inside, Ryder released a small whistle and gestured for Wolf to follow him. The dog gave a pitiful howl and looked at the door before turning sad eyes toward Ryder. He stifled a laugh. The dog looked how he felt. Like he'd lost a friend. Only Cara wasn't his friend. They had shared a few minutes of civility and adult conversation, and he wouldn't confuse friendliness with friendship. They were acquaintances. Nothing more.

Chapter Four

Chanel stood on her lawn, which was littered with leaves of orange and yellow from one of the large trees in her backyard, rubbing her arms and watching a couple of rabbits race across the expanse. She was dressed in a thick cream sweater, jeans and boots that were wet from the morning dew.

A mosquito buzzed by her ear. She swatted it away and wiped her brow, glad she had remembered to apply the Skin So Soft this morning. The little pests seemed to love feasting on her brown skin. Though it was November, the weather was still in the low seventies, which prolonged the mosquito season that usually ended in October or during the first freeze.

While she drank her second cup of coffee, she reflected on her activities over the past seven days. First, she had fixed Cara's vegetable garden, but she knew the small wire-welded fence she had put in wouldn't keep the rabbits, deer or Wolf out for long.

Next, she had finished the exterior Christmas decorations, adding a couple of reindeer and another snowman on the lawn. Chanel had ordered a wreath for the front door. Every time she came home and inhaled the pine scent, she had to smile.

And finally, she had cleaned and organized the house—a habit developed from working in the library. She had read about ten novels. Yes, ten. She was a fast reader and enjoyed posting her thoughts about the books on an online review site. Chanel had toyed with the idea of opening a bookstore, but so many independent bookstore owners she knew had ended up closing because of significant loss of income.

Instead, Chanel had decided to volunteer at the library. She glanced at her watch. She had an appointment with the local librarian, Mrs. Nora Madden, in about thirty minutes, so she should have already been on her way.

Lifting her face, she soaked in the morning sun and scanned the open field before her. It was time to till the land to make it yield fruit and profit again.

She sighed and turned her back to the yard before going inside to put her coffee mug in the sink and grab her résumé. She made sure to secure the back door, frowning when it jangled. The locks needed to be switched out.

After deciding to do that after her meeting, Chanel headed into town.

Once she had parked in front of the huge building, Chanel took a moment to admire the large, new library. The automatic doors made a satisfying swoosh as she sauntered inside. There was a staircase to the second floor on her left. In the middle, a door led to an atrium. Chanel could see herself sitting out there, surrounded by greenery and sunlight while she read.

To her right was a children's nook with a book checkout not too far away. Her brows rose at the self-checkout area. This new library exceeded what she had experienced as a child. Noting that she was ten minutes early for her appointment, Chanel wandered into the children's alcove. There were books about fall on display, a DVD section, a large reading area with a mix of small and large couches and chairs, and a small play area. A couple of toddlers sat playing with a bead-maze toy, tugging it between them while their mother shushed them. All they did was giggle.

Chanel laughed at their antics. She felt a light tap on her waist and jumped before looking down. It was Gabby.

"What are you doing here?" Gabby asked, holding a couple of picture books in her hand. "I didn't have school today, so Daddy bought me here so I can look at books."

"You mean *brought*, not *bought*," Chanel corrected. Stooping to look Gabby in the eyes, she said, "I love coming to the library." Her heart twisted at the earnest expression on Gabby's face. Something about this little girl just warmed her insides and made her ache for something more. Something she couldn't have.

"But this section isn't for grown-ups." Gabby's voice was loud in the otherwise quiet of the room.

"I know, but I love reading stories to the children. And don't forget to put your inside voice on, okay?"

"Okay," she said, nodding, her voice solemn.

Ryder approached, wearing a black turtleneck, black jeans and brown boots. "Fancy meeting you here," he said, eyes twinkling, holding on to the strap of a laptop bag on his shoulder.

"Dad, can I go play with the beads?" Gabby asked, loud enough to draw attention. Chanel bit back a laugh.

It was obvious Gabby had already forgotten about using her inside voice.

Gabby stood with her chin in the air, looking up at Ryder with such trust that Chanel had to bite her lower lip to keep from melting and cooing, "Awww."

"Sure, but keep your voice down. And let me hold those books while you go play." Ryder patted Gabby on the head, his eyes following when she ran over to play with the toddlers, a grin on his face.

"I came to volunteer, keep myself occupied," Chanel said once Gabby had squatted to the floor. She curled her fingers around her purse to hide the discomfort she still felt a week after expressing such intimate feelings about her only child and chance at motherhood. Ryder was a stranger, and Cara wouldn't share personal details of her life with her neighbor—or anyone, for that matter. Since that day, she had avoided Ryder, his dog and especially his daughter.

Not to say she didn't watch Gabby frolicking in the yard with Wolf. But though her feet itched to go outside and join them, Chanel stayed rooted on the other side of her door.

Hibernating. Hiding.

"Ah… I see." His eyes widened before he gave a little nod. "Have you decided when you'll be able to help with Wolf?" His tone was friendly but neutral. Safe.

Ryder had sent her a text to ask about the dog training, but she had told him she needed a few more days to get herself together. Chanel knew she couldn't stall anymore.

"How about tomorrow?" she asked, her heart thumping in her chest.

"That sounds good." He pierced her with a gaze. "I

read about what happened in the paper, with that computer hacker and how you resigned."

She lowered her eyes, hating the deception and small-town news. "Yeah, I hate that he's free because of my mistake."

He tilted his head. "That's not the way I see it. Neither does anyone in this town, for that matter. We see you as a hero—or rather, heroine. You've got to know that."

Her head popped up at the compassion and slight awe in his voice. "What do you mean?"

"The only reason Jeremiah Greene escaped is because you stopped to help a pregnant woman in labor. Debbie would've lost the baby if it weren't for you. So cut yourself some slack."

She stifled a gasp. That was the mistake? Cara was too hard on herself. She hadn't told Chanel all of that. Chanel vowed to scour the newspapers for more details.

Realizing Ryder anticipated a response, she said, "I guess."

"No 'I guess.'" He tucked her under the chin. "You're one person, and if no one else tells you, you made the right choice."

Her heart squeezed. "Thanks for saying that." Her eyes became glassy as she thought of how driven her sister was to solve this case. How filled with guilt. It was nice to know the people of Hawk's Landing didn't share the same perspective.

He ran a hand through his hair. "I'm sorry I made you run off the other day. Or was it last week? The days seem to blur into one another."

Chanel blinked. "No need to apologize. I was... overwhelmed." Then she remembered she was playing a role and couldn't lose character, so she cleared her throat and hardened her tone. "But, as I said before, I'd prefer to leave the past in the past."

His face reddened. "I'm sorry. I shouldn't have brought it up. It was just that…ah…well, you seemed so…sad."

Oh, if only he knew it wasn't just this conversation that made her feel on edge. That was a small part. The greater part was him. She liked his company. Felt more alive than she had in years. But she couldn't dishonor her husband's memory. Not when he had died trying to save her.

"I'm good," she said. Glancing at her watch, Chanel could see it was time for her interview. Tucking her bag under her arm, she said, "If you'll excuse me, I have to talk with the librarian." But even as she put distance between them, Ryder and his daughter infiltrated her thoughts more times than she could count.

What some called nosiness Ryder called curiosity, and he had an abundance of that. Curiosity was a necessary trait in his field of work—but not in regular conversation.

If he were thinking, he wouldn't have brought up the topic of her child, for whom it was obvious Cara still grieved. Key words being *if he were thinking*. But he hadn't been. He had been admiring her long lashes splayed across her cheeks like a fan, and her ready smile. And Ryder had caught the tender look she had on her face while observing Gabby.

So that's why Ryder had asked the question, and also to keep from hugging her, consoling her about a past that time hadn't eased.

He tapped his chin. He knew a lot about that kind of pain. The damage inflicted by his parents hadn't lessened. Their betrayal had left a gap, a chasm he had worn like a trusty blanket until he met a love big enough to fill any open space: God's love. He hadn't known it at the time, though.

He would have still been carrying that torn, tattered blanket of pain if it weren't for a random internet search. One night, on impulse, he'd typed "how to overcome past pain" in the search bar. A YouTube video by Pastor Shawn Johnson called "When Past Hurts Still Hurt" popped up. That video was the beginning of him changing his life. If he hadn't accepted Christ, Ryder knew he wouldn't have been able to take care of Gabby. He wasn't sure if Cara was a woman of faith, but that didn't mean he couldn't share his faith with her.

He moseyed over to sit on one of the couches and then put his laptop on his thighs to look up the video in his saved files. From his vantage point, he could keep an eye on Gabby while watching out for Cara.

Gabby ran over to him. "I'm hungry, Daddy," she shouted.

He gestured for her to lower her voice. "We'll get something to eat in a few minutes."

"Okay," she said, her shoulders drooping. "But I'm really, really hungry."

Quirking his lips, he thought his daughter had never looked cuter, but he repeated, "In a few minutes." He patted the books and asked if she needed another one. Gabby loved to read and to be read to, so Ryder wanted to encourage that.

She poked out her lips. "I'll go find another book." Then she scuttled down a nearby aisle.

Ryder clicked through his bookmarked sites until he found the video. He took out his AirPods, placed them in his ears and pressed Play. Twenty minutes later, after

Ryder had fielded Gabby's questions about when they would eat at least ten more times and checked out her picture books, Cara came out of Mrs. Madden's office.

Hurrying to his feet, Ryder grabbed his laptop and books, then rushed over to catch her before she exited. Gabby was right next to him.

"You're still here," Cara said, eyebrows raised. Her eyes darted back and forth, like she was in a hurry to leave or trying to escape him.

Normally, Ryder would take that as a cue and just let her go, but he wanted to be in her presence, though he wasn't sure why. He enjoyed being on his own, but he just knew that he liked her energy, her personality, when she shared herself with him.

"Yes, uh, I was waiting for you." He sounded hesitant, unsure, even to his own ears.

She tilted her head, her eyes narrowed. "Why are you waiting for me?"

Ignoring the frost in her tone, Ryder said, "I wanted to show you something."

"What is it?"

"Daddy, I'm hungry," Gabby interjected.

"I know, honey," he said.

"I'd better let you go," Cara said, taking a step back. She looked like a deer, shy and ready to run.

Adjusting the items in his hands, Ryder squared his shoulders and gathered his courage. "Why don't you come to lunch with us?"

Shaking her head and giving Gabby an almost fearful glance, Cara said, "I can't. I have to check on something at home."

"Is it something I can help you with?" he asked. "I can grab pizza and meet you at your house. I'm pretty handy."

"You're real persistent, aren't you?" she asked with a little laugh.

"Yes, I can be when I really want something." His heart hammered. She'd said he was persistent, not pushy. He saw that as a plus. Nevertheless, since he didn't want to turn her off, he added, "I enjoy your company, and I wanted to share something with you."

"The lock on the back door is loose. I've got to repair it before it gets too late. I won't be able to sleep tonight if I don't get it done."

"I can help you with that," he said, glad it was something he knew how to do. "I'll stop by the hardware store and get you a Master Lock."

Her answering smile brightened her face, and Ryder had to look away to keep from staring. "Tell you what— since you're getting the lock, I'll get the pizza."

"Yay! I love pizza," Gabby said, twisting this way and that.

"All right, see you in about a half hour." It wasn't until he and Gabby were in his vehicle that Ryder realized he had a huge grin on his face. All because of Cara. He frowned and self-corrected. If he was smiling, it was because he was about to eat pizza. Not because he was about to eat with his neighbor. He just loved pizza.

"Are you mad, Daddy?" Gabby asked.

Her question jarred him into action, and he pulled out of the lot. "No, honey. Just thinking about something." Or rather, thinking about *not* thinking about someone.

"What? What are you thinking about?"

"Pizza."

"But why would pizza make you mad?"

Why indeed?

Chapter Five

On her drive home, Chanel replayed Ryder's account of her sister's "failure." Cara was being really hard on herself, and Chanel intended to tell her that whenever she spoke with her. She gripped the wheel.

But then again, she was also hard on herself. Her therapist had told her that several times, urging her to forgive herself.

That wasn't easy, especially since she didn't want to.

Not after the loss she had caused.

Cara had urged her to date again, open her heart, but Chanel refused. How could she move on when Warren was frozen in time, forever young? When her child had gotten to know only the walls of her womb and had never taken a breath? There would be no more deep relationships in her life if she could help it.

If Cara hadn't been insistent, sharing God's Word and His love constantly, Chanel would've retreated into herself and into her guilt, and possibly cut her sister off. But Cara was more stubborn than she was. In time, Chanel's faith had been restored, but she was determined to remain unattached, embracing singlehood. And it was enough.

But when she closed her eyes, all she saw was Gabby. The pull was easy, magnetic.

And it scared her. She really needed to stay away.

Yet here she was, turning into her driveway with an extra-large order of pizza, honey-BBQ wings and a brookie. Everything sat on top of a book Chanel had checked out of the library for Ryder to read to Gabby.

Seeing that Ryder's truck was not in either of their driveways, Chanel decided to set up their dinner outside on the lawn, picnic-style. She strode into the house with the pizza and the book, which she placed on her coffee table. Then she grabbed an oversize red-and-white-checkered blanket, utensils, napkins, cups, plates and some bug spray before setting everything up on the grass. Realizing something was missing, Chanel ran into the house and grabbed the cushions off the kitchen chairs. Then she laid them out.

That's when Ryder appeared with Gabby, her little arm curled around his arm.

He held tools in one hand and the door lock in another. How…domestic. Her throat tightened. For a second, she struggled to catch her breath.

"A picnic!" Gabby yelled. She broke free from Ryder's grasp and began to run, her little legs pumping fast. Before Chanel could react, the little girl was against her chest, hugging her tight.

Inhaling, Chanel caught a whiff of baby powder and closed her eyes. Her arms ached to wrap themselves around Gabby's small frame, but she held back. Instead, she patted Gabby's hair and pulled away.

"You like picnics?" she asked, slightly choked up.

Bobbing her head, Gabby plopped onto one of the pillows and scooted close to her. "Yes, I love picnics."

By this time, Ryder had arrived and squatted on the pillow on the other end of the blanket.

"What do you like about them?" she asked the little girl, forcing the enthusiasm to cover her sudden nervousness at having Ryder so close.

Curling her tiny hand around some of the checkered cloth, Gabby said, "I've never been to a picnic, actually." She rocked her legs like a butterfly. "But I always wanted to do this for a long time."

"Yeah?" Ryder chuckled. "How long?"

"A billion years," Gabby shouted, lifting her hands in the air as Chanel cracked up.

Chanel put on some insect repellant, then passed it off to Ryder. It was late in the season but she wasn't taking any chances. First, he applied some on Gabby's arms and ankles since she was dressed in jeans, a T-shirt and a zippered sweater; then he did the same for himself. It was close to seventy degrees, and the sun made it feel even warmer. Once he was finished, they went to the outside pipe to wash their hands.

After blessing their food, Ryder chose a small slice and a couple of wings and placed them on Gabby's plate, reminding her to say thank you.

Then he waited for Chanel to get her slice before he reached for one. She admired his thoughtfulness. The only one missing was Wolf.

"Where's Wolf?" she asked before biting into her pizza.

"He's at the high school, getting a wash, trim and his nails clipped."

"Sounds luxurious," she said.

"You're telling me. The football team did the pet wash as a fundraiser."

"Great idea," Chanel said.

"Daddy does the same for me all the time," Gabby chimed in. Again, her voice was at a louder-than-necessary pitch. Chanel knew about that. She clasped her hands, resisting the impulse to touch her ear and her implant. After the accident, she had lost her hearing in one ear. That's the reason she kept her hair down; the townspeople would know she wasn't Cara if she revealed it.

She laughed. "It must be nice to get such special treatment," she said to Gabby.

"Daddy can do the same for you," Gabby almost yelled, looking at her father. "Right, Dad?"

A splash of red hit both his cheeks. "No, uh, Ms. Cara doesn't need my help," he stammered.

Hearing her sister's name gave her a jolt. Chanel had forgotten her charade just that fast. She had been about to tease him, make him more uncomfortable, but his calling her Cara stilled her tongue. Cara had a different sense of humor. Her sister was more literal, so she would not respond by poking fun at Ryder.

Chanel poured some juice and took a sip, choosing not to say anything. Instead, she changed the subject. "So, what did you have to show me?"

"Ah, yes, I almost forgot." He told Gabby to go play since she was finished eating, then wiped his mouth with a napkin and pulled out his phone. After clicking and swiping a few times, he cleared his throat. "When you were speaking earlier, about losing your child—"

She held up a hand, cutting him off. "I told you that topic is off-limits." She eyed Gabby, who was doing flips on the lawn.

"I'm not asking you to talk about it," he said. "I know we're not…friends, per se, but I wanted you to listen to this message that helped me, uh, overcome a lot. I can text you the link."

Her eyes went wide. "A message?"

"Yes, if you don't mind."

She shook her head and wiped her hands on her jeans. "Send it to me."

With a nod, he complied. A second or two later, her cell pinged. She pulled it up and read the title, "When Past Hurts Still Hurt."

Her eyebrows shot up. "This is a little presumptuous, don't you think? Like you said, we're not friends. Just neighbors sharing a slice or two. That's it. That's all it can ever be."

"I'm not—I'm not looking for anything...more," Ryder said, rubbing the back of his hand across his forehead. "But you said to me that you thought it was all your fault, like you caused your daughter's death, and so I—"

The words *daughter* and *death* in the same sentence slashed open the guilt that she'd tried to keep under the surface.

Chanel jumped to her feet, stuffed her phone in the back pocket of her jeans and began gathering the picnic paraphernalia to keep from lashing out. "You think a handful of conversations give you the right to butt into my personal life?" She regretted ever saying anything to Ryder.

"Cara, please calm down," he asked gently. "I meant no harm."

Deep within, she knew that. So she drew in a heavy breath and exhaled. "I'm sorry. I know you mean well, but I'm not comfortable discussing my child with you. Or anyone." Her voice broke. "It hurts too much. It's been years, but the pain is still very real to me."

Gabby ran over to say she needed to use the bathroom, and Ryder opened his Home app to unlock the front door. Once she was out of earshot, he spoke.

"I understand a thing or two about lingering pain." His tone implied that he really did. Staring off into the horizon, Ryder continued, "When I was nine years old, on Christmas day, my parents took me to the movies. I was so excited because they didn't always have extra money to do anything since my father worked as a cook at a diner and my mother was a receptionist."

He flailed a hand. "Anyway, they took me inside the theater and told me that they were going to get popcorn and they'd be right back. I remember nodding, my eyes glued to the screen because I didn't want to miss anything. For a couple hours, I was caught up in the movie, and I wasn't concerned when my parents didn't come back right away."

His pain was unmistakable.

She gasped and shook her head. "No. Don't tell me…" Chanel's heart twisted. She dabbed at her eyes and placed a hand on his forearm.

He clamped his jaw shut and shoved his hands into the pockets of his jeans. "That day at the movies… That day was the last time I saw them."

Overcome, Chanel could only whisper, "I'll watch the message tonight."

He hadn't spoken about his abandonment in years.

Ryder sat by his fireplace with Wolf curled at his feet, looking into the ashes of a fire past. After he'd changed the lock on Cara's back door, Ryder and Gabby had headed to the school to get Wolf; then he'd spent the rest of the day talking his colleague through their research project. The guy was practically begging him to come back to work, but thinking of Gabby, he wasn't ready.

Ryder had tried calling Brittany, but she hadn't responded. He had felt helpless seeing Gabby's tear-streaked face. Every attempt he made to boost his daughter's spirits had been unsuccessful. By the time he'd put her to bed, his mind and body were worn out. When he wasn't fretting about Gabby, he was occupied with memories of the most defining event of his life.

Once he'd begun talking about it to Cara, it was like peeling back time. Ryder felt all the emotions accompanying being left in the movie theater at nine years old. First, the bewilderment, then the fear as he rushed in and out of all the theaters in the building, screaming for his parents. When the police were called, he'd cried and kicked, not wanting to leave. He had wanted to wait for his parents.

Parents who never returned, never left a note, never said goodbye. He'd searched for them a few months before his thirtieth birthday, but his efforts had been unsuccessful.

That was a pain he had carried with him for most of his life—along with the fear. Fear of being abandoned by someone else he cared for. He kept loose associations with people, never letting anyone close. He held fear and pain in both his hands, his partners for most of his life. After that video, he'd released the pain and had accepted God into his life. But the fear—the fear remained. Like the ash and soot in the chimney, remnants of a past fire, his fear coated his heart, dictating all aspects of his interactions, keeping everyone at a distance.

He went to church online. He worked in a small lab with few coworkers—all as emotionally detached as him. He lived alone in a remote location. Purposeful selections. Ryder had enjoyed the solitude.

Until Gabby.

Gabby was the only person to pierce through that veneer. His heart had been no match for her innocence. Her mother had left her with him, a virtual stranger, promising to give Gabby the best Christmas ever upon her return. Not that Gabby saw him as a stranger. Before bringing Gabby to meet him, Brittany had shown her pictures and talked about her daddy, which helped Gabby accept him with ease. However, she missed her mom. He knew that sadness in his daughter's eyes because he had felt it himself. Ryder had let her in, though he feared losing her when Brittany returned. He loved Gabby with a fierce protectiveness that surprised him. In learning to care for her, he had begun caring for himself.

He had let Gabby in. Then Wolf. And now it seemed as if his neighbor was next. Ryder rubbed his chin. It was mind-boggling how Ryder craved Cara's company. Okay, maybe *craved* was too strong a word. He spent hours talking to a five-year-old and needed adult conversation.

Wolf jumped to his feet and barked, his tail wagging.

"What's going on, boy?" Ryder asked, scratching his ears. "You need to go outside?"

Just then, the doorbell rang.

"Oh, you knew someone was coming." Ryder smiled. "You're a good guard dog." He stood, stretched and went to see who was at his door. It was a little after nine—too late for a package delivery, not that he was expecting anything.

When he opened the door, Cara stood outside, holding a book in her hands.

"Hey, neighbor," she said. "I hope I didn't catch you at a bad time."

"No. No. I just put Gabby down, although she wore me out," he said, stifling a yawn.

"Oh, I see. Sorry to barge in without calling or texting first. I forgot I had a book I wanted to share with you." She waved the book at him. "I checked it out of the library for Gabby. I think she'll enjoy it."

"Oh, great. Thank you. Come on in." Ryder opened the door wider and stepped aside to let Cara inside his home.

"Are you sure? You look ready to call it a night."

He was, but he wasn't about to admit that. "Yes, I'm sure. I'm good."

She hesitated for a moment before stepping through the door. On the outside, Ryder kept his features composed, but on the inside, he marveled.

His cranky neighbor was in his home. Wolf circled her, dancing a jig with little hops. Celebrating the monumental moment. Besides himself and Gabby, Cara was the first person to cross the threshold who wasn't a worker installing appliances or delivering furniture.

Laughing at Wolf's antics, Cara looked around. He watched her take in the fireplace, the mantel lined with Gabby's pictures, the large throw rug, the green sectional, Wolf's mat—which had his name engraved in all caps—and his chew toys. Ryder kept a neat home; cleaning and dusting were a regular part of his evening routine. Though he was too tired to do that chore tonight.

He wondered if she noticed there was no television. He avoided them and going to the movies.

"You have a nice place," she said, handing him the book. "I haven't been in here since I was a kid."

"Thank you," he returned. "I've restored this level, but I still have upstairs to deal with. The stairs need to be redone, and I have to renovate the bedrooms. Gabby's room might get drafty in the winter, so I'm going to get a consult to see if I need to replace the windows next."

"Yes, I replaced all the windows inside my house a couple years ago," Cara said. "And my wraparound porch could use some reinforcement—but as the saying goes, 'There is no place like home.'"

"Exactly, so you'd better take care of it."

They shared a laugh, then a moment of awkward silence before Ryder ushered her to the sofa and they both took a seat. Wolf jumped into her lap and closed his eyes.

Perched on the edge of the sofa, Cara held up the book. It had a picture of a little girl with a beautiful Afro. The title was *I Am Enough*. "It was written by Grace Byers, and I think Gabby will like it."

"Thanks so much. I'll read it to her tomorrow." He reached over to take the book out of her hand, their fingers touching briefly. Ryder felt a light zing and wondered if she had felt the same electrical connection. But, of course, he wouldn't ask her that.

Cara cleared her throat. "I watched the video. It was really inspiring. Gave me plenty to think about. Thanks for recommending it to me."

"I thought so too," Ryder said.

"I can't imagine going through something so horrible as a child," Cara said, broaching the subject of his parents' abandonment. "I don't understand how some people get the gift of children and then don't care for them, or abandon them. Some of us would do anything to have had children." She shook her head. "It all seems so unfair."

He could hear the pain in her voice and knew she was thinking of her own situation. It was obvious she yearned to be a mother.

"That very question bothered me for most of my life," Ryder acknowledged. "For years, I blamed myself. I wondered what I had done to make my parents leave me like that."

She patted his hand. "You were a child. You did nothing wrong."

"I know that now, but I still have scars that I carry with me for life." He pointed upstairs and whispered, "I didn't plan on having children because of that pain, and I had been careful to ensure that didn't happen."

Cara gave him a small smile. "That means Gabby was meant to be here." She tilted her head and asked, "By the way, have you noticed she tends to speak at the top of her lungs?"

He nodded. "Yes. I have to tell her all the time to lower her voice. I don't know what that's about."

Licking her lips, Cara averted her gaze from his. "Um, have you thought about getting her hearing checked? I'm no expert, but I do know that speaking at that volume could be a sign of hearing loss."

His eyes went wide. "No. I didn't even consider that."

"I—I've had some experience with that, so that's the only reason I would think of it."

The way she said it made it sound like a personal experience, but with Cara being such a private person, Ryder knew better than to push for details. He didn't want her shutting down or leaving.

"I'll make an appointment with Dr. Wallen tomorrow to get her hearing checked."

"Good." She released a breath and fiddled with her

hair. "I was nervous to suggest it—but at least rule it out."

"Well, I'm glad you did."

She shifted and stroked Wolf's fur. The dog had fallen asleep on her lap. "Well, I probably should be going. I'm supposed to start volunteering at the library tomorrow, a couple hours in the afternoon. I'll be doing a kiddies hour three days a week, but other than that, I'm open."

"That sounds wonderful. I'll bring Gabby to the kiddies hour. I'm sure she'll be excited about that. How long does it last?"

"Great. The more, the merrier. It shouldn't be longer than ninety minutes. Mrs. Madden was going to put up signs and email her subscriber list so they know about it." Her brows furrowed. "Why are you asking?"

"I'm planning to visit the John Dickinson Home. I know it was a plantation, but I love looking at old architecture. I wanted to see if I had enough time to go and be back in time to get Gabby."

"Oh, you'll enjoy the tour. It's a historical landmark converted into a museum. There's even a building on-site that's a replica of enslaved-people housing—plus, of course, the mansion."

He arched a brow. "You're a history buff?"

"More like a wannabe history buff," she countered with a shy laugh.

They had a lot in common, Ryder thought. They enjoyed the same music, loved dogs and now they shared an appreciation of history. Those were a good start to a friendship.

"Unless you want to come with me?" He regretted the words as soon as he had uttered them. Ryder lifted a hand. "Scratch that question. I got caught up for a second." He thought he saw relief in her eyes, so he rambled on. "I'm just glad we started being more than a wave—or rather, more than argue buddies. I think you're pretty cool, and so does Gabby. I can see how comfortable she is with you, and you know how Wolf feels," he said, pointing at dog on her lap. "It's safe to say that the members of the Frost household are Cara fans."

Cara gave a quick nod. "I think you guys are cool as well. And if you're okay with it, I'll keep Gabby until you return from the museum."

"Sounds like a plan."

She held out a hand. "I hereby declare us…friends?"

He accepted the handshake. "Friends." Then he stood and lifted Wolf off her lap. The dog appeared to give Ryder a mean glance, then headed toward his mat.

She sauntered toward the door before whipping around. "See you tomorrow, friend." Then she was out the door.

Ryder watched her go, his chest feeling light. Cara would be good for Gabby. And though he would pull a front tooth before he admitted it, she was also good for him.

Chapter Six

Chanel slipped a few pieces of chicken jerky into her sweater pockets. She had texted Ryder to bring Wolf over with his leash once he had placed Gabby on the bus. It was a much cooler morning, so Chanel had dressed in a thick purple tunic, black leggings and boots. She had also placed a steaming carafe of coffee with two mugs on the small glass table, in case Ryder decided to stick around for the lesson.

While she waited, Chanel read a novel she had started the night before and sipped on her coffee. From her vantage point, she could see Ryder bound out of the house, towing Gabby in his arms and running to catch the bus, which she had heard pull up. He was wearing a dress shirt under a sweater vest and a pair of slacks. Wolf, on the other hand, raced over to where she sat reading.

"Hey, boy," she greeted Wolf, placing her book on the table and ruffling his fur.

He stood panting, his long tongue hanging from his mouth as he sniffed the air. She cackled. The pup must be smelling the jerky in her pockets. "You'll get plenty of treats if you're a good boy during our lesson today."

Ryder had forgotten to put on Wolf's leash like she'd requested, but Chanel figured she would begin anyway. She stood and guided Wolf to the middle of the porch. Ryder came into view, and she gave him a quick wave.

"I'll be by soon," he shouted. "I've got a conference call."

"No worries. I've got this."

Wolf began circling her and jumping and barking. He did that three times before Chanel captured his attention with a piece of jerky. She commanded him to sit and touched his nose. That made Wolf lift his head and sit. Then she gave him a treat.

"Good boy," she said. She repeated that twice.

Wolf ate the treat, then barked, panting in anticipation of more jerky. In a firm tone, she ordered, "Sit." Chanel raised her hand—palm facing upward—touched his nose, waited for him to sit and then fed him jerky. She practiced this over and over until all she had to do was lift her hand and Wolf would sit. Each time, she praised him and rewarded him with a treat.

"Good boy," she said, patting his head. "You're so smart. You'll be trained in no time."

Wolf barked and Chanel cracked up. She leaned over to rub her nose against his, his warm breath fanning her face. "You're not easy to resist, you know that?"

"Am I interrupting?" came a voice from behind her.

Chanel shrieked and straightened, almost losing her footing. "Ryder, what's up with you sneaking up on me? You've got to give a girl more warning."

Ryder chuckled, lifting both hands, one of which held the leash. "I'm sorry. I couldn't resist. Wolf is obviously lapping up all the attention and loving it."

She snickered. "Jealous?"

"Maybe," he teased, waggling his eyebrows.

Wolf barked and then emitted a little howl, as if complaining about Ryder stealing the focus from him. Chanel signaled for him to sit and then fed him the last of her treats. Ryder applauded.

"Impressive. I can't believe you got him to do that in less than an hour." He gave her a look of admiration that accelerated Chanel's heart rate a bit too much.

Chanel pointed to the coffee to cover her reaction. "Help yourself if you haven't had a cup. Judging by your sprint to the bus stop, I'd say you'd had an eventful morning."

"Gabby was in rare form. She refused to eat breakfast. She didn't want to wear her sweater and jeans, insisting she would be warm in her tutu." He shook his head. "I don't know what happened to my sunny child of the past four months."

Ryder looked defeated, and her heart went out to him. Chanel wrapped her arms around herself to keep from giving him a hug. "She's five and her tooth has been hurting, right? Did you give her any pain medicine? Orajel would be good."

"No, it's loose. I didn't think that would hurt."

"Are her gums red?" Chanel asked. "If so, that can be really uncomfortable. Or she could be getting some new teeth. You never know."

His cheeks reddened. "I should have checked."

"It's all a part of parenting," she said in a soothing tone. "So quit feeling guilty. I'm sure by the time she's in school, she will be back to smiling and laughing."

"I hope so." Ryder looked apprehensive.

"You can always email her teacher and ask for an update."

He brightened. "Thanks. I'll do that." He tilted his

head. "You're really good with knowing children's needs."

Chanel shrugged. She had learned a lot by being a librarian and running the children's corner. But of course, Ryder wouldn't know that. "I'm not an expert. Just guessing. For all we know, I could be way off base."

"Somehow, I doubt that you are." His eyes narrowed. "I'll pick up some Orajel for her gums later. Thank you."

They shared a smile. She felt a warmth in her heart that had nothing to do with the coffee, which scared her.

"You would make a great mother," Ryder said, breaking the spell.

Her heart squeezed as her thoughts flashed to Warren and their daughter. Chanel tore her gaze away from his. She had stood on this very porch with Warren, sharing many tender moments, yet all she could visualize right now was Ryder's wide smile.

That wasn't good.

That wouldn't do.

Panicked, she breezed out a quick goodbye and escaped into her house. Though she had prayed for God to heal her past pain, the guilt still remained, wearing her down. She dashed for her cell phone to call Cara and tell her that coming back here had been a mistake. She needed to leave this house, this town, and return to Virginia.

Her call went to voice mail.

With a yelp of frustration, Chanel drew in deep breaths. Lifting both hands and looking upward, she called out, "Why did You bring me here? Why am I back in this town?" Her chest heaved. Since returning, her dreams had intensified. She woke up sweating, having relived the details of that fateful day in her sleep.

Her cell phone pinged with a notification. It was You-

Tube, sharing another message on past pain and hurt. Not knowing what else to do, Chanel slumped into the chair and pressed play.

After Cara ran off because of his thoughtless comment, Ryder returned home with Wolf to work in his office, feeling slightly deflated. He wanted to text Cara to check on her but decided to give her space.

After calling Dr. Wallen to make an appointment and emailing Gabby's teacher, Ms. Hyland, Ryder reviewed the results his colleague had sent of the latest research. Even though he was out of the lab and not actively involved in the research, he still wanted to be noted as the lead researcher on the project they'd been working on when he left. It was his idea, his hypothesis, his research method—his everything. His name being first on that article would be a big deal. Especially if it ended up being the breakthrough they hoped it would be.

Finally, he stopped and rubbed his eyes. There was something wrong with the results, but he couldn't figure out what. And he really wanted to. Needed to. Any contribution he could make toward cancer research would be meaningful to so many, and he was glad to make a difference. Ryder paused. He had his answer. He'd been questioned about his plans for returning since taking leave during the conference call, but he had been unsure. But now he knew he would return after the New Year. This was what he was meant to do.

Eyeing the clock, he saw it was close to Gabby's arrival time. He dashed outside to warm up his truck and then raced through the front door, bounding through the living room area and walking toward the back of the house to his kitchen.

Wolf howled, so Ryder took a moment to pour food and water into his bowls.

Grabbing his backpack from the back of one of the kitchen stools, he checked to make sure his iPad Mini and Apple Pencil were fully charged so he could take pictures and make notes for his visit to the John Dickinson Home. He also prepped some healthy snacks—carrots, celery and cheese cubes—before deciding to make some beef-pastrami sandwiches. He could eat while he toured. Ryder packed everything into his oversize lunch box and added some bottles of water.

Hearing the screech of the school bus, Ryder jogged to stand by the closed doors. He liked to be there when Gabby got off the bus. She usually jumped the last two steps into his waiting arms. When the doors whooshed open, his heart pounded. The little girl he had sent to school had been crying, and his heart would ache if she came off the bus the same way.

Thirty seconds later, he saw her little face, and she had a wide smile. With a yelp, she yelled his name and lunged into his arms. Ryder swung her around and asked, "How was your day?"

"Good. I'm going to be the caboose next week," she said.

He scrunched his nose. "The caboose?" he asked. The word *caboose* made him think of a freight train. A caboose was generally located at the rear so he asked, "Does that mean you're last in line at school?"

"I don't know," she said, shrugging her shoulders. He opened the rear door of his truck to strap her into her car seat.

"Where are we going, Daddy?" she bellowed.

"I'm taking you to the library for the kiddies hour. You'll be with Ms. Cara until I get back."

"Yayyyy." Seeing his daughter's bright face gave Ryder pause. She must really like Cara, which was a good indication of his neighbor's sweet nature.

Gabby's long legs dangled over the car seat. He was probably going to have to get a booster chair. But since she would be leaving in a few months—something he dreaded—he hadn't made the purchase. He closed the rear door and went around the vehicle to the driver's side.

When he was backing out of the driveway, his daughter rambled on about her day. "Daddy, guess what?"

"What, sweetie?"

"Rayshawn really wanted that job, but Ms. Hyland said I was going to be caboose."

"That's great, sweetie."

Of course, once they arrived at the library, Gabby made sure to mention it right away to Cara, who was waiting for them in front of the entrance. They stepped to the side to allow other patrons to enter.

"Oh, my. That's really exciting," Cara said, smiling. "I think you'll make a great caboose. I used to love when I got to be the line leader."

"Me too," Gabby beamed.

While Cara and Gabby chatted, Ryder furrowed his brows. Cara seemed to know a lot about children for someone who wasn't a mother. She had spent most of her life as a police officer, then a detective. While she'd mentioned she used to work in a pet store, she hadn't said anything about working with children. But she did volunteer at the library, and she obviously loved children.

For all he knew, Cara could have worked in a preschool or with the children at school. Ugh. He really needed to let this go. He was thinking too much.

Putting an end to his musings, Ryder addressed his daughter. "How was your tooth today, Gabby?"

"Oh, yeah, I forgot to tell you—my tooth came out!" Her voice echoed in the library. "Ms. Hyland said she was going to email you."

Slapping his forehead, Ryder released a breath. He had forgotten to check his personal email after sending the note to her teacher. "I'll look at it later." At that moment, he doubted his parenting skills. He needed to set the notifications on his devices so he wouldn't miss any communication about Gabby.

"Wow. You lost a tooth," Cara said with wide eyes. "You know what that means?"

Gabby wiggled and squealed. "What does it mean?"

He saw Cara discreetly tap her ear and asked Gabby to speak at a lower volume. Of course, that wouldn't last. "It means you're becoming a big girl."

"Yep. I didn't even cry when it came out." Gabby puffed her chest. "I bit into my sandwich and *pop*—it flew out onto the table. The other kids jumped up." She laughed. "I had to go to the nurse with my partner, and Mr. Lin made me wash my mouth. He put my tooth in a baggie for you."

"You've got to show me your tooth later," Cara said with excitement.

Ryder's heart warmed. Every day with Gabby showed him something new about parenthood. He enjoyed seeing life through her eyes.

After glancing at his watch, Ryder kissed Gabby on the cheek and told her he would be back soon.

Cara glanced at Ryder. "I can take Gabby home if you want."

"Thank you. I appreciate that. Let me get her car seat."

Once he had dropped off the car seat, Ryder rushed

over to the plantation. Once there, he marveled at all he saw and took copious notes. Just as he was about to depart, Cara texted. I will be on my way home soon.

Thanks. See you in a few, he texted back, and then left the plantation.

Since Ryder arrived home before they did, he answered Ms. Hyland's email, checked Gabby's backpack for her homework and then decided he would read her the *I Am Enough* picture book Cara had brought over.

The front door slammed, and Gabby bounded inside. Ryder went to close the door and, with a wave, yelled, "Thank you," to Cara, who was already backing out of his driveway.

Then he settled with Gabby to read the story. He was immediately drawn to the little girl dressed in overalls, a white T-shirt with yellow polka dots and what looked to be Converse sneakers on the very first page. Wolf came to sit by them, his ears cocked like he was listening.

Gabby loved it so much that she began to act out the scenes from the pictures. Ryder cracked up watching her try to fly like a bird, do a handstand and execute a karate kick like the little girl in the story. He loved the message of the child believing in herself and loving others who are different. One of the lines about living a life of love and not fear resonated within him. Was that what he was doing? He wasn't sure.

Pushing that thought aside, he finished the story. Gabby clapped her hands and asked him to read it again, which he had no problem doing because he had enjoyed it too. Ryder planned to ask Cara for more suggestions.

He read another story about pumpkins and asked Gabby if she wanted to visit the pumpkin patch. The months of October and November were pumpkin-picking time.

"What's a pumpkin patch?"

"It's a huge farm where they grow pumpkins."

"Oh, I want to go get a supersized pumpkin," she yelled, pumping her fists, her eyes shining and bright. "Can we go tomorrow?"

"I don't know. I have to check the Fifer Orchards website to see if there are still tickets available tomorrow." He met her eyes. "Now, I need you to know that they may not be open. So, if they aren't, we'll have to go another time."

"Okaaaay." She drew out the word, sounding bummed.

He hated to see her downturned face. "If they are open, I'll reserve our tickets, and we will definitely go tomorrow."

Since he didn't have a television, Ryder encouraged Gabby to play with her dollhouse and toy kitchen upstairs in her bedroom. He had assembled them during her second month with him, and she spent hours playing house. Ryder had been invited to many of her tea parties.

Taking the stairs two at a time, he walked down the short hallway to the master suite to retrieve the Mac-Book Pro he'd left on his bed. Pulling up the Fifer Orchard's website, he was glad to see they were open until the end of November. Ryder chose an early time for the next day and purchased tickets to the pumpkin patch. Seeing there was also a corn maze and a fun park option, he bought combo tickets to those activities as well.

"I got us tickets to the pumpkin patch," he yelled to Gabby.

She ran into his room and gave him a wet kiss on the cheek. "Yay!"

Ryder truly enjoyed being able to help her experience many firsts. His heart squeezed as he thought about other potential firsts—her first bike ride without training wheels, her first date, her first prom—that he would miss once she was gone. But he couldn't dwell on that. Instead, he would make sure to do all he could for her now.

When Brittany called, they would work something out.

He hated to hope—his parents had taught him not to do that—but he still did. There was no denying his daughter's place in his life and his heart. Maybe Brittany would agree to joint custody. He didn't want Gabby thinking he'd abandoned her the way he had been abandoned.

Chapter Seven

Maybe this was a sign she needed to leave the sweets alone. Chanel had gotten dressed early, intending to visit Ms. Collins's shop again to stock up on more treats and to order some of her special Christmas cookies. It was a few minutes after six a.m., and her stomach was already awake. Not for one second did Chanel imagine that the car wouldn't turn over when she tried to start it up. She blew out a breath of exasperation and texted Ryder. Sorry to bother you but my car won't start. Can you give me a jump?

His response was immediate. Sure. I'm on my way.

While she waited, Chanel googled for the nearest mechanic and found Luther's Car Stop and Shop. If the car started, she would head straight there for him to check it out. She prayed it was the battery and not the alternator or the transmission that was wrong with the Honda.

Chanel fought the temptation to trade in Cara's hooptie for a new vehicle on a daily basis. Her sister was as attached to this car like gum on carpet, so Chanel would make an effort to get it repaired. But if it was the transmission, then she would have to get new wheels because Chanel wasn't about to keep asking Ryder to assist with her transportation needs.

She saw that Luther's opened at eight o'clock, and Chanel planned to be one of the first to arrive at his shop. The Honda had stalled on her way to the library yesterday, but Chanel had pressed on because she hadn't wanted to disappoint the children. Four children had shown up, and watching their faces light up with wonder at her storytelling had given her immense pleasure. Purpose.

Ryder's truck swerved into the spot beside her.

She could see Gabby's little head bobbing and Wolf in the back seat. Ryder exited the vehicle, leaving his driver's door ajar. Chanel opened her car door since she wasn't able to roll down the windows.

"I'm sorry to be an imposition."

"It's not a worry at all," he said. "I hadn't even started breakfast when I got your text."

Now she felt additional guilt because Gabby must be hungry. "Please let me treat you to breakfast," she offered. "I can order delivery. That's the least I can do for putting you out."

"Cara, you didn't put me out. Gabby can eat breakfast at school. It's fine. Trust me." He gestured for her to climb out of the car. "Let me take a look and see what's going on."

"It won't turn over. That's why I think it might be the battery," she offered.

He adjusted his long legs and slipped into the driver's seat. Then he stepped on the brake and turned the key. The car made a chugging sound and then went dead.

"Let me give it one more try," he mumbled, and turned the key again. This time it didn't even make a sound. Ryder got his jumper cables and tried to give her a jump but he was unsuccessful. He sighed. "It's completely dead. I don't think it's the battery. I'll call to have it towed."

Allowing Ryder to do all that would blur the lines of their friendship. He had already purchased a new lock for the door. And she had too much of an independent spirit to let him take responsibility. "It's okay. I'll arrange to have it towed."

He raised a brow and got out of the car. "Are you sure? Because I don't mind in the least." Ryder pressed the lock, but nothing happened, so he locked the door manually and held out the key.

"Yes, I'm sure," she said with a quick nod. She reached for the key. The electrical charge when their hands touched gave her a warm tingle.

"All right," he said.

Chanel smiled, pleased he didn't see her as feeble and helpless.

"Ms. Cara, your car's not working," Gabby shouted. Chanel turned to see Gabby's mouth covering the top of the window.

"That's dirty, Gabby," Ryder said.

"I'm pretending to be Wolf." She yelped a couple of times, but she did remove her tongue and lick her lips.

"You're not a dog. You're a child," Ryder said. "I park my car under trees, and birds can poop on it."

Chanel scrunched her nose at that thought.

Ryder continued, "So no more putting your tongue on the window—or on anything else, for that matter. Got it?" He paused and waited for Gabby to answer.

Gabby opened her mouth like a fish, nodded and then closed it. She lowered her head, her face stained with red.

Chanel was proud of how Ryder had handled the

situation. He was respectful, loving, but firm. And he took the time to explain why he didn't want Gabby licking the window. "You're a good father," she whispered so Gabby wouldn't hear.

She almost cracked up at the shock that registered on his face.

"Thank you. That means a lot. I don't know what I'm doing almost 99.9 percent of the time, but I know my love for Gabby was instant and it's immeasurable. I almost wish I could quantify this emotion, but there would be no number big enough to adequately express what I feel for that little girl."

Wow. Chanel touched her chest. "What a love." She understood the depth of love that Ryder described for Gabby. She had felt it when she was pregnant with her little girl and that's why the loss had been unimaginable. "I wish I could experience even a small percentage of that again."

"You can," he said.

She furrowed her brows and watched him sprint around to his side of the truck to talk to Gabby and after a beat, she joined him.

"I'm hungry, Daddy," Gabby said, reaching over to pat Ryder's back. Wolf barked, like he was echoing Gabby's sentiment.

Chanel chimed in. "Remember, I'm buying you breakfast."

Jutting his jaw, he said, "You're not obligated to return the favor."

Her lips quirked. "As your friend, I am more than capable of buying your family a meal, because it makes me feel good to do that. Understand?"

"All right," he said, relenting. "Thank you."

She pulled up Grubhub on her phone and ordered

their meal using Ryder's address and name as contact on the order. It would arrive in about twenty-five minutes. Jumping inside his truck, Ryder returned to his home so Gabby could finish getting dressed for school. Chanel walked over once she had used the bathroom and called for a tow truck. The driver promised to get there a little after seven-thirty.

Sitting at Ryder's kitchen table, she drummed her fingers on the tabletop and asked a question on her mind. "Just now, when I said I wished I had experienced that kind of love with a child of my own, you said I could. What did you mean by that?"

"I meant you could always choose to adopt. Open your heart to a little girl or boy."

His quiet-spoken words hit her heart with a geyser-sized force, causing all the emotions bottled inside to pour out. Her mouth opened and closed while she strove to find the strength to respond.

Clamping her lips, she lowered her head, hating the tears that streaked down her face. She turned to look out the window, desperate to hide the fact that she was falling apart.

Once again, Ryder had said the wrong thing. He really needed to keep his mouth shut or at least consider his words before he spoke. Tossing out the suggestion that she adopt a child like it was as easy as flipping pancakes or navigating the zero-turn lawn mower on her lawn was insensitive. And could be perceived as judgmental.

He could hear Cara's light sniffles, but he didn't know if he should pretend not to hear or if he should simply apologize. This was why he avoided relationships—er, friendships—and stuck with research. But it seemed as if God wouldn't allow him to be like Jonah, alone in the belly of the big fish.

He went upstairs to help Gabby get dressed for school, giving Cara some privacy to compose herself.

"I have to go to the bathroom, Daddy," Gabby whined while he brushed her hair.

"Go ahead," he said, hearing the doorbell ring.

Cara was already at the door when he descended the stairs. She tipped the delivery driver and turned to him, holding their food.

"I'm sorry about earlier," he said, taking the food out of her hands.

"Don't worry about it," she said, not meeting his eyes. She walked past him, heading toward the kitchen. Gabby came down the stairs and raced to grab Cara's hand.

Seeing their hands together, Ryder's breath caught. They could be mother and daughter. Yes, they were different races; but for him, parenthood transcended race. It was a connection, a love, independent of color. One he had never had with anyone once his parents left.

He blessed their food, and they had breakfast, laughing and joking like a family. And it was easy. Effortless.

Gabby soaked up every bit of attention that Cara offered, and it made his heart squeeze. He was grateful for their rapport but also a little fearful. Cara was a friend, nothing more, and he didn't know if he should try to limit her interactions with Gabby. He didn't want his daughter forming an attachment and starting to imagine them as one unit.

It was evident that his daughter was missing her mother, and Brittany hadn't been in contact since she left. He vowed to renew his efforts to reach her. That would keep Gabby from getting confused.

Despite his concerns, Ryder loved having Cara around. He would just make sure to reinforce that they were only friends so Gabby wouldn't think anything else. Unless he was overthinking things…

"Are you coming pumpkin-picking with us after my school today?" Gabby asked, dipping her French toast sticks into a blob of syrup.

"Uh… I don't know, but I bet you're going to have a lot of fun." Cara fiddled with her hair, then slid a glance his way like she was waiting for him to say something.

"Aww. I want you to come," Gabby yelled. She turned her baby blues to Ryder. "Daddy, can Ms. Cara come?"

"She might be busy, honey," he said after a brief pause. He took a sip from his second glass of lemonade.

Great. That made it sound like he didn't want her to come. He did. Ugh. If only he could get out of his own head. He was trying to give Cara an out if she needed one. Ryder didn't want her feeling manipulated into spending time with him and Gabby.

"Yeah, I, uh—I have to look after my car," Cara said.

"Okay," Gabby drawled out with a pout.

The thing was, Cara didn't seem relieved. She remained quiet even as she walked with them to Gabby's bus. So quiet that he could hear every breath she took. He couldn't tell if his hesitation had hurt her feelings.

"Thanks for your help this morning," Cara said, twisting her fingers together. A light breeze made her hair fly in different directions. "I'm going to the mechanic early, but I can give Wolf a lesson while you both go to the pumpkin patch if you want."

"I want you to come." The words flew out of him.

Her eyes went wide. "Really? I thought you felt I was imposing."

"No, I don't at all. I like being around you—probably too much. Cara, I value our friendship, and Gabby thrives in your presence. I want you to go with us, but I didn't want you to feel pressured into saying yes."

Her eyes misted. "I'd love to come. I'll get my ticket tonight." She touched his sleeve. "You asked me earlier why I haven't considered adopting before, and—"

"Hang on," Ryder said, holding up a hand. "I should apologize again for that heedless comment. Feel free to tell me it's none of my business. That was way out of bounds."

"I don't mind your asking, because I believe you did it with the best intentions."

Just then, they heard a loud whoosh of someone pressing on the brakes. The tow truck had arrived, and the owner was backing into Cara's driveway. Ryder knew their conversation would have to continue another time.

She cleared her throat. "I'd better go, but I will say this. The reason I have never adopted is because for years, I could only picture myself having a child—biological or not—with my husband, Warren. When he died, I buried my dreams of motherhood with him." She wrapped her arms around herself. "Frankly, I don't deserve to be a mother."

Chapter Eight

Luther shook his head. "I don't think it's worth the fix. It's gonna cost you more to get the car running than its value." Chanel had made it to his shop at a few minutes after eight, having hitched a ride with the tow truck driver and thankfully, Luther didn't have a customer so he had taken a look at the car right away. He rolled his chew stick to the edge of his mouth and stuck out his gut, making his paunch more pronounced under the overalls.

Though the outside temperature was close to fifty degrees, Luther wore short sleeves. Her lips quivered, but he didn't seem to notice the sharp gust of wind.

She shielded her eyes from the sun's glare and met his gaze. He was about an inch shorter than she was. "So what do you recommend I do?"

"Buy yourself a new one, or get you a good used car. I have a couple Hondas similar to this one out back with less mileage, and their CARFAX reports say one owner and no accidents. If you want, I can give you the trade value for this car because I could use the parts."

Chanel hadn't thought about getting a newer used

car. It didn't hurt to check out Luther's inventory. The car dealership wouldn't open for another hour anyway.

Scrunching her nose, she said, "Let me take a look at what you have." She hoped to find one the same color and style. Her heart thumped in her chest. Cara wasn't going to be happy about this, but Chanel didn't have a choice.

Stifling a yawn, she followed Luther to the rear of the building. There were about ten cars of various models in different states of repair. Some had sale prices posted in the window, and some looked like they had been stripped down for parts. Judging by the tossed oil cans and empty packages, cleaning wasn't a priority, and Chanel had doubts about the condition of the cars.

But both Hondas were covered with tarp, so that was a good sign. Chanel was picky when it came to cars.

The first one was a weird neon green. It wasn't a glossy green either; it looked matte. She made a face and shook her head. He took off the tarp over the other, and she gasped. She walked around the vehicle. It was blue-gray and in mint condition. No marks, no blemishes and it had leather seats. She clapped her hands. "I'll take it."

"Told ya you'd like it. It's the sports version, and it's manual." He grinned, showing a chipped front tooth.

Her smile dimmed. Really? He should've started with that. Chanel knew how to drive a stick shift because Warren had taught her, but Cara hadn't learned. Unless she had in recent years. Chanel couldn't text or call to find out.

Shoving her hands into the pockets of her watertight jacket, she asked, "What else do you have in good condition?"

Luther scratched his head. His strawberry curls were

sticking up in all different directions. "The only thing I have is a pickup truck. It's automatic, but I doubt you'll be interested. You can check back in a week or two, and I can see what else comes my way."

Her brows rose to her hairline. "I want to see the pickup," she said, excited.

With a shrug, Luther removed the tarp, and when she saw the truck, her stomach clenched. It was a burgundy Ford F-150 Super Cab. "How much is it?"

He quoted her a price well within her budget, calling it a pre-Christmas sale. She didn't hesitate. "I'll take it."

"You don't want to test drive?"

"I'll drive it out the lot now," Chanel said. For her, this pickup truck was a sign. It would be perfect for farming, which Cara had been urging her to do. She had decided to start tilling the earth by her sister's vegetable garden to widen the space. Start small and then spread out. Chanel planned to consult with the farmers at Fifer Orchards when she went to the pumpkin patch and purchase some seeds. Volunteering at the library for an hour or two wasn't enough to fill her days, and restoring the garden would be a great Christmas present for Cara.

Chanel needed to be exhausted at the end of the day, and expanding the garden would do it. Voicing her deepest guilt to Ryder had left her shaken, and she didn't want time to think or dream about Warren and her loss.

She would start her farming project; then, when she left, Cara could hire another hand or sell the house as a working farm. Either way, it would be a win.

"Cara?" Luther called out, shaking her back to the present. "Let's go get the paperwork for both vehicles taken care of."

Oh, no. She was supposed to be her sister. How was

she going to sign off on the papers? She looked at her watch. It was now after nine o'clock, which meant the bank across the street was open. "Um, if it's all right, I'll pay cash and you can sign the car over to me. Since I have to get to an appointment, I'll take care of getting it registered myself. And are far as the Honda, if you tow it to the junkyard, I'll fill out the paperwork and fax it over to them."

He narrowed his eyes like he was sizing her up. Chanel kept her gaze firm, hoping the promise of cash would quash the questions. After a beat, Luther spat out his chew stick and said, "Suit yourself."

After jogging across the street, Chanel withdrew the cash from her account without any difficulty and then paid Luther. With that done, she drove over to the next town and took care of all the necessary paperwork at the DMV, registering it in her own name. She could transfer ownership to her sister later. The pickup was a smooth ride, and Chanel knew Cara would love the truck. A couple hours later, Chanel backed into her driveway, the truck bed filled with supplies she would need to begin working on a patch of the lawn. She felt exhausted but satisfied.

Ryder must have been looking out for her, because he ambled over as soon as she cut off the engine. She didn't want to think about how much she felt uplifted because of his welcoming smile.

Cara had officially been added to his prayer list. Though she had watched the YouTube videos, when Cara had said she didn't deserve to be a mother, Ryder realized she was hearing the words but not able to truly listen.

Her past pain was too heavy.

The Scripture "Cast your cares on Him" had been on the tip of his tongue to recite, but Ryder held back. Cara knew she could do that, and he didn't want to appear as if he were chastising instead of encouraging. Instead, he had prayed for God to help him be the friend and support she needed. He was so glad they had moved past their squabbles and were getting to know each other.

Ryder had sat on his porch, reading and studying his Bible while waiting for Cara's return from the mechanic. Once he saw her pull into the driveway, he hurried over.

"Nice truck." Eyeing the soil, garden tools and wiring in the back, he asked, "Need help with that?"

"Would you?" she said, opening the cab door.

A hyena couldn't have smiled wider than he did as he hoisted the bag of soil onto his shoulder. Ryder had expected Cara to brush him off—she was so independent. But she had willingly accepted his help, which meant she trusted him. Or it could be something simple—like she wasn't foolish enough to turn down the offer. The bag weighed at least sixty pounds; she could injure herself lifting it. And there were two bags.

She went ahead of him, carrying the grass rake, shovel and fencing.

"What are you planning to do?" he huffed out.

"I'm going to expand the garden," she said. "I'm starting small, but I want to work my way through the entire yard. Grow things."

"You're becoming a Jill-of-all-trades," he teased, plopping the soil on the spot she pointed out.

She chuckled. "I guess you could say so. I'm trying to fill my days." Cara wiped a hand across her forehead, leaving a trail of dirt.

"Don't run yourself ragged. If you need my help, just

ask. I'm more than willing to pitch in, especially since Wolf has made a mess of your yard more times than I care to mention." He kept his tone light. "You have dirt on your face."

He reached over to wipe her forehead with his thumb. Like he would do for Gabby. He stilled. Only this *wasn't* Gabby. This was a fully grown woman standing before him. He moved his finger, grazing her cheek. "It's all gone now," he whispered.

"Thank you," she breathed out, averting her eyes. "I'd better go wash my face and hands."

She skittered into the house while Ryder crooked a finger in the pocket of his jeans and surveyed the yard. This was a lot of land she planned to till. Even though she had a good strategy, it was a lot for one person to do alone. Even for two or three, it would be backbreaking work without the proper machinery and equipment.

"Do you plan on getting any equipment?" he asked once she returned.

"They are in the shed," she said. "I just have to get some gas and see if they still work. But I don't need them now with what I plan to do."

"I'll help you," Ryder found himself offering again.

"You don't have to."

"I know. But I want to."

She opened her mouth like she was going to turn him down but then shook her head. "I hope you know what you're getting into."

He didn't, but he marched to the front to get the other bag of soil. It was close to Gabby's arrival time, and their reservation for the pumpkin patch was in an hour, so Ryder planned to fix them a quick lunch and then be on their way.

"Did you eat yet?" he asked.

"I grabbed a turkey sandwich, so I'm good."

He heard the squeal of the bus before he saw it. Ryder dropped the soil in the backyard and then sprinted down the driveway to meet Gabby. He didn't expect Cara would be running beside him.

They stood together when the bus stopped. The doors opened, and Gabby scuttled down the steps. Instead of jumping into his arms, she made a beeline for Cara and hugged her around the waist. He watched Cara give his daughter an awkward pat, and his heart constricted.

Cara and Gabby became immersed in conversation, trailing Ryder into his house. He prepared stove-top macaroni and cheese while listening as they rambled on about their day behind him. They sat together at the kitchen table, and Gabby showed Cara her homework assignment. It sounded like she had to do subtraction with pumpkins and color in the answer. Cara gave her gentle guidance, and he was pleased at her patience. The more he listened, the more he knew Cara needed to be a mom.

Ryder would have to think of a tactful way to broach that option again. There were a lot of singles who had adopted, and Cara was capable and efficient.

"Can I get a ride in your truck?" Gabby asked.

"Sure, if your dad agrees."

"Can we go, Daddy?" she asked, her little voice wrapping its way around his heart.

"I don't mind, but it can't be today because we already have plans."

Gabby responded with her usual drawn-out, "Okaaaaaay…"

He was glad his back was turned, because the way she said the word, along with her down-turned lips, always got to him. He had a hard time not caving.

But Cara must have been in Gabby's direct line of vision, because she said, "Ryder, maybe we can take my pickup, if you don't mind driving? I can sit with Gabby in the cab if that's all right. There are two seat belts back there."

Hiding his grin, he said, "That's fine by me."

"Yay!" Gabby shouted.

"You are a punk," he whispered in Cara's ear.

She rolled her eyes and gave him a playful shove but didn't deny that Ryder was right. Instead, she asked him about Gabby's doctor's appointment.

"Oh, yeah. Dr. Wallen's office called me early this morning and rescheduled for tomorrow. They said a new mother gave birth, and he had to go provide a consult on the baby, who had trouble breathing."

"Oh, wow. I hope the baby's okay. I'll say a prayer."

"I did the same thing as soon as I heard," Ryder said. The more he was getting to know this woman, the more he found her remarkable. Her initial response echoed his own. His brows furrowed. They shared common interests in music, dogs, history. But for the first time, he wondered at the many similarities between them. Maybe they weren't just coincidental. Maybe they were a sign of something…more.

Chapter Nine

Watching Gabby's eyes shine with excitement and wonder as they walked through the pumpkin patch gave Chanel a thrill. And an ache. There were a few other families present with children running in circles around the pumpkins.

Gabby pointed, her eyes wide. "Look at that really big pumpkin!"

"Yes, some can grow way bigger than you. Did you know that you can eat the pumpkin flowers?" Ryder asked.

Her mouth popped open. "Wow. No, I didn't know that. So if I eat it, I won't get a bellyache?"

Ryder touched her curls. "Nope. It's safe to consume."

The little girl grabbed Chanel's hand, which gave her a jolt—in a good way. This is what it would have been like if she were out with her own child. She smiled, giving Gabby's hand a slight squeeze.

"Go stand by the pumpkin," Ryder said, holding up his phone. "I want to get your picture."

"Okay." Gabby ran to do his bidding. Placing a hand

on her hip, she stuck a leg out, tilted her head and smiled wide. Her father took several shots.

Chanel bit back a grin at the supermodel in the making.

"Come, Ms. Cara," she said, gesturing with her little hand. "Take a picture with me."

Chanel went to her side, and Ryder moved close to them, holding the phone at an angle to capture all three of them. A lady passing by offered to take their picture. Ryder, Chanel and Gabby huddled close and posed.

"You guys are a beautiful family," she said, handing back the phone.

Chanel didn't bother to correct the woman. "Thank you," she said instead, flipping her hair. To her surprise, Gabby did the same, which made Chanel's heart turn to mush.

Ryder's eyes met hers. He must have seen Gabby mimicking her actions. "You caught that, right?" she asked.

He gave a light nod and grinned. "She's been doing that since we got here. Copying your moves."

Aww. Gabby's sweet innocence warmed her heart. Loving that little girl was as easy as cotton candy dissolving on her tongue—a silly analogy brought to mind by the enormous amount of pink cotton candy Gabby had consumed once they hit the corn maze and fun park.

Lying in bed that night, staring up at the ceiling, Chanel couldn't recall the last time she'd had so much fun. Plus, she had taken care of a little bit of business, talking with the farmers to get tips and also purchasing various winter-hardy seeds for her garden. Once she had completed her purchase, Chanel had rejoined Ryder and Gabby in the pumpkin patch, and they had carved pumpkins.

Gabby was a joy. And Ryder…

It had been good to see him relaxed and not so serious. When he did, he was pretty cool. Thinking of Ryder brought his suggestion of adoption back into her mind. Maybe she should look into it…

No.

There was no point in feeding hope.

Hanging out with Gabby and volunteering for the children's hour at the library would have to be enough. Becoming a mother was a lifetime commitment, and maybe that wasn't in God's plan for her. The last time she had made a long-term commitment led to devastation. A devastation that continued to haunt her dreams, no matter how much she crammed into her day.

Her eyes fluttered closed, and she welcomed the exhaustion. Perhaps tonight, she would sleep without awakening in a cold sweat.

She'd prayed and asked God for deliverance, but what if this was her penance for her husband dying because of her actions?

God may have forgiven her, cast it in His sea of forgetfulness, but Chanel remembered. It lingered below the surface, dictating all her actions.

Her sister called it survivor's guilt. And it gnawed at her like a field mouse on grass. No matter how much she replayed the events of that day, Chanel couldn't understand why God had spared her and not Warren.

Why?

Ugh. She squeezed her eyes tighter and focused on the night sounds. The crickets… The frogs… Ryder. His thoughtfulness. His humor. His ability to spout off random facts about pumpkins.

How pumpkins were a staple food worldwide. How pumpkins and humans share about 75 percent DNA. In less than hour, she had heard terms such as *genome* and *Cucurbita* and had more than her fill of the fruit-squash.

Still, her inner nerd thought his earnest sharing of all that knowledge was cute.

No, Chanel. Stop it. She didn't need to be thinking about Ryder. Especially since Ryder thought he was talking to Cara. Cara, not her. Well, she was being herself—most of the time—but he didn't know that.

When they had done a little pumpkin carving and he'd wiped pumpkin from her forehead with such tenderness, she had wanted him to see *her*. Not her sister. Though they were carbon copies. Ugh. She massaged her temples. It was complicated, but if she were talking to Cara, her sister would understand what she meant.

Cara would get Chanel's need to be seen and understood as an individual.

Her phone pinged with a message from a blocked number: Your sister got hurt. Not serious. Will check in when possible.

She popped up in bed, her heart racing. Chanel sent Cara a text, though she didn't think she would receive an answer. She reread the text, dissecting what was said and not said. *Hurt.* Not *dead. Hurt.* Not *dead.* She had to believe that. Nevertheless, Chanel began to pray.

Lying on her side, curled up in a fetal position, worry, fret and fear rolled around her stomach like tumbleweeds. She clenched her teeth to keep from crying out. Chanel couldn't lose another person she loved. She knew she wouldn't be able to survive it. How she wished sleep was an abyss into which she could fall.

"Gabby shows signs of fifty percent hearing loss," Dr. Wallen said.

Those words weakened him, and if he hadn't already

been seated, Ryder's legs would have folded like an old Chinese fan. Gabby sat playing with the trucks in the corner of the room, talking and singing. She loved to sing and dance.

"What caused it?" Ryder croaked after swallowing. He hated the thought that something was wrong with his child and he hadn't known it. If Cara hadn't mentioned it, Ryder wouldn't have thought to have her hearing evaluated.

"It could be a number of things. Possibly an untreated infection, if her hearing was normal at birth," the doctor said. "I would hate to speculate without reviewing her medical records."

Ryder shifted, averting his eyes and focusing on the picture of a winter scene from Candy Land. The office had been decorated for the winter season, with actual gifts under the Christmas tree. Someone had posted a sign that said they were collecting presents for needy families for the holidays. Ryder's immediate thought had been *What about the rest of the year?*

Realizing the doctor expected a response, he offered, "I've emailed her mother to find out her history and to get her primary physician's contact information. I didn't think to ask for those things."

But he should have. Ryder couldn't use the excuse that he had never been a father before. He was a researcher, a scientist. Most of the answers to what he studied were in the past. The past was a window to the future.

If the doctor was judging his incompetence, he said nothing. Instead, Dr. Wallen made a note. "If you do get information, please forward it to me. In the meantime, I'm going to refer you to an ear specialist." He proceeded to write a script.

"Will she completely lose her hearing? Or will she require surgery?" he asked in a low tone so Gabby wouldn't overhear.

"In most cases, hearing aids are all that's needed. But the specialist will be able to provide guidance after taking a look at her ears. I'm also prescribing something to get rid of the buildup. She might experience some discomfort, and you can give her ibuprofen as needed."

Ryder released a shaky breath. Even his hands trembled. Dr. Wallen led them out front and past the reception desk to wait for the paperwork. Gabby chattered along the way, her face bright and unsuspecting.

"Are we going to the liberry?" she yelled. A huge reminder of her hearing difficulties.

"Yes, but we've got to get our *li-br-ary* books first." He drew out the correct pronunciation of the word.

Agitation and worry churned within him like an angry washing machine. He felt helpless and unsure. That feeling stayed with him all the way home. Gabby raced up the stairs to get her library books. Praying Brittany had received his email, Ryder went into his office, Wolf on his heels, and checked his inbox to see if she had responded.

Nothing. He slammed a hand on the table, causing Wolf to yelp in alarm. "Sorry, buddy. I'm just so frustrated." He rubbed the dog under the ears, which gave him a small measure of comfort.

"I'm ready, Daddy," Gabby said, clutching her books.

Seeing her standing there with her missing tooth, smiling from ear to ear, made him choke up. He cleared his throat and gathered her in his arms, holding her tight as she wriggled.

"Let's go, Daddy," she said, her voice booming in his ear.

Using all his willpower, Ryder planted a smile on his face. He led Gabby down to his vehicle and tickled her to make her laugh as he settled her into his truck. He gripped the wheel tight as he held on to the emotions threatening to engulf him. Worry for his little girl filled his belly as well as concern for her mother. Something major had to be going on with Brittany for her not to reach out to her child. He had to believe that. Ryder refused to entertain the notion that she had abandoned their daughter.

And if that were the case, he didn't know how he would tell Gabby. Okay, he was getting ahead of himself. At this point, no news was good news. That had to be his mantra.

When they walked into the library, Ryder was surprised to see about twenty little ones sitting at Cara's feet while she read. She was like the Pied Piper of the town. All the children had rapt expressions on their faces, and the parents milled about the room, looking just as entranced. Gabby almost jumped out of his arms and scampered over to the join the group.

Cara gestured for Gabby to join her, and Ryder's heart tripped when he saw she had left a small spot open for her. Gabby scooted as close she could, her head upturned so she could see the picture book.

Ryder turned to hide the sudden mist in his eyes. After learning about his daughter's hearing loss, he had tried to reach Brittany, someone he believed cared about Gabby.

But he also could have called Cara.

Ryder was thankful to God for bringing her into his life, because he needed to talk. To pour out all he was feeling.

He marched over to the front desk to return the library books before he forgot. Then he set off into the stacks to find a few books on hearing loss, though he would also dig through the job's research site later. It gave him something to do rather than stand and stare at Cara and Gabby.

Ryder located a couple texts of interest, but then he found he was as eager to listen in during the story time as the children. He settled into one of the armchairs so he could read and observe them from a distance.

Cara sat by the window, the sun illuminating her animated face and those freckles splattered across her nose. Her passion for storytelling and her voice characterization made the hour a treat. Parents applauded right along with the kids. And Ryder found himself mesmerized by the ease with which she interacted with the young ones. She listened attentively to their questions and comments.

For a brief second, she looked his way and smiled. His breath caught and his eyes became glued to hers. They connected. His insides calmed. Then she looked away, and he wondered if he had imagined that fleeting moment.

It didn't matter anyway because she was devoted to her dead husband—and more importantly, they were friends. That was all he needed now more than anything. That was all he could offer because anything more for him was out of the question. He wasn't about to put himself out there to anyone and get rejected.

At the end of the story hour, Gabby and another little girl ran to the girls' restroom. Parents circled, wanting to talk to Cara. He watched, bemused. When she was a detective, she had been so unapproachable. But since she had resigned and left that career behind, it was like she had been transformed into a different person. Ryder could testify about her change firsthand.

Cara had avoided him, his daughter and his dog for months. And now she was becoming—had become—part of their lives. Though he welcomed it, he was also terrified. Terrified of her switching up on him again and hurting Gabby.

The families dispersed and Cara made her way over to him. Gabby came out the bathroom and went to sit at one of the tables which had picture books on display. Cara had on a flowy skirt, boots and a turtleneck. Her jacket had been stuffed into a large bag hanging on her shoulders.

"You are a chameleon," he said once she was in front of him.

"What do you mean?" she asked, scrunching her nose.

"I mean you're a natural with children, and you might have found your calling or a second career. When you resigned, I imagined you would get into private investigative work or something. I wouldn't have guessed you'd find pleasure in volunteering at a library. It just didn't add up to the person I knew—or *thought* I knew." That's why, deep down, he didn't believe he could trust her. She was too much of an enigma. Too much of a risk.

Her eyes went wide. "I…well… There's more to me than what you see on the surface," she stammered, fretting with her collar, her cheeks flushed.

"I don't mean to embarrass you, but I wonder if I have misjudged you. In my head, I saw you as my temperamental neighbor. I had no idea you were so…different. It's jarring. It kind of makes it difficult for me to trust my judgment. Because how could I be so wrong about you?" He stopped because Cara now appeared quite uncomfortable, averting her eyes.

"Stop," she tore out, a myriad of emotions on her face. "You don't have to say anything." Her eyes pleaded with him to drop it.

He saw Gabby get up from the table and dart down an aisle and knew he had better get going but Ryder needed to finish expressing himself. "Let me say this." He squared his shoulders and took her hands in his. "You, Cara Shelton, are wonderful. Getting to know the real you has been the best thing that's happened to me, aside from meeting Gabby."

Tugging out of his grasp, Cara dabbed at her eyes. "I, uh, thank you…" she trailed off, shaking her head and biting her lower lip.

Doubt about their friendship reared. Maybe she didn't like being around him, which wouldn't be a surprise since his parents hadn't wanted him around either. He stepped back as uncertainty wielded cords around his mind. Maybe she was too nice to voice the truth. Her mouth hung open like she was unsure of how to handle his declaration. He stiffened under the silence.

"I've got to check on Gabby." Ryder stomped off, wondering what it was that made people ice him out once he opened up.

Chapter Ten

Now why did she have to freeze up like that? Cara slammed her bag onto the truck outside the library, fighting the dueling urges to cry and scream. She had spent most of the day anxiously trying to reach her sister until she'd finally received a cryptic text saying Cara was okay.

Hearing that had put her at ease, causing joy to bubble over that at least her sister was alive and safe. After offering prayers of thanksgiving, Chanel had poured all her relief into entertaining the children.

Not once did she consider that it would make Ryder marvel at her transformation. She slapped her forehead. She was supposed to be Cara. She was supposed to behave the way her sister would. But she had gotten caught up, and she had forgotten the role she was playing.

After getting into the pickup, leaving the door ajar, she rested her head on steering wheel and acknowledged the real reason she was upset.

Guilt.

Guilt was like a vine growing inside her and taking over her body. Ryder had called her wonderful, but that's because he didn't know. He didn't know the big lie she was living, pretending to be Cara. And as she stood there and listened to him talk, all she felt was fear. Fear that had her quaking, shaking, at his reaction when he learned the truth.

"Chanel?" a voice called out. One she recognized.

Her stomach twisted and her heart raced as fast as kids running out to recess. "Excuse me?" she asked, ducking her head.

"I knew it was you." Ms. Mavis, the former librarian, approached. "I heard that Cara was holding a kiddies hour, and I had to come. Imagine my surprise when I saw you had done a switcheroo." She wagged her fingers and cackled. "Did anyone else figure it out?"

Chanel gave a light shake of her head, then gasped. Ryder had exited the building, holding Gabby's hand. Her heart thumped and she drew rapid breaths. "Ms. Mavis, I hate to be rude, but… I have to go."

Thankfully Ryder was far enough away that he wouldn't hear their conversation but she had to get out of there. Chanel turned on the ignition, hoping Ms. Mavis would get the hint.

"We've got to catch up," the other woman said, pushing her glasses up the bridge of her nose. Chanel didn't want to be rude, but her hands were shaking. And he loomed closer. She could hear Gabby yapping.

Even closer.

Sweat beaded across her forehead. She released a breath. "I've got to go. Please don't tell anyone."

Ms. Mavis scrunched her nose. "Okay… But why?" She placed a hand on Chanel's arm. "Are you in trouble, dear?"

Great. Gabby had spotted her. "N-n-no. I—I've got to go. Ms. Mavis, I'll call you tomorrow." Giving her a wave, Chanel tore out of the space before making herself slow down—there were parents and children walking to their cars. Safety trumped her fear of being discovered.

Once she had turned for home, she released a sigh. That had been a close call. But the fact was that Cara wasn't going to be gone forever.

She would return and the charade would end. The curtain would fall. Then Chanel would have to see the hurt and pain from her betrayal on Ryder's face.

Some would argue this lie was necessary. She was doing it to protect her sister. But a lie was still a lie. And she wasn't only lying to Ryder. She was lying to Gabby. That sweet little girl who looked at Chanel with such love and trust was going to be confused and hurt, even if she couldn't articulate it.

Oh, this was all a mess. She needed to pray.

Ever since Chanel moved in, she had felt the urge to create a prayer closet—a special place to pray. But she hadn't because, though she had spent so much time there as a child, the house didn't feel like her home. She felt like she was intruding in her sister's space. However, Cara expected her to make the place hers. Her sister believed God wanted Chanel to move here permanently.

And maybe it was time she embraced that. Her heart raced and all sorts of doubts plagued her mind, but Chanel was willing to explore that option. Maybe instead of resisting her past, she needed to begin to use it to fuel her future.

If she got the farm working again, sustaining a profit, that would honor Warren's memory and, perhaps, give her enough peace to sleep when she closed her eyes. The idea was far-fetched, but she was willing to try.

For some reason, the biblical history of Naaman came into her mind. Naaman had leprosy and needed healing. But when the prophet told him to dip into the River Jordan seven times, all he did was complain at first. He saw the river as dirty, as beneath him, though it held his second chance at life.

Fifteen years had passed since Warren's death, and Chanel had done a lot of crying and praying, but her deliverance hadn't happened. Maybe the farm was her River Jordan. She needed to get her hands dirty by working with the earth to kill the seeds of guilt and bury the hurt and pain so that there was a chance for new growth. Hope.

Chanel was tired of restless nights. She was sick of toting around this backpack of past hurt when all it was doing was weighing her down. She wanted to be the woman Ryder saw in her.

After making a quick U-turn, Chanel rushed to the hardware store to purchase paint and then to the town's craft store. Then she went home and cleared out one of the two small closets in her bedroom. After giving the room a good vacuum, she gathered the lilac paint she had purchased.

Next, Chanel placed a small prayer bench in the room and affixed a cork board about two feet above the floor. She used pop-out letters to spell out the words *Prayer Closet* on the wall. After decorating her journal with print paper, glue and ribbon, Chanel rested it on the prayer bench. Leaving the door open while the paint dried, she slipped to her knees and dedicated the space, then offered up praises to God. An hour later, she closed the door behind her, feeling refreshed.

Checking her phone on the nightstand, Chanel decided to text Ryder. In her panicked state, she had forgotten to ask how Gabby's appointment went. Good evening. Just reaching out to ask if Gabby saw Dr. Wallen today?

She didn't know if he would respond, and she wouldn't blame him if he didn't. But her concern outweighed her angst. She waited, hoping to hear a ping. Yes. He referred me to an ear specialist. Dr. Wallen says she could have as much as 50 percent hearing loss.

Her eyes went wide. Wow. Poor Baby. What does that mean?

She will have to go to a specialist. I have an appointment the Monday after Thanksgiving. I can't thank you enough.

Her brows furrowed. For what?

For suggesting I get her hearing checked.

Oh...you're welcome.

She waited for a good five minutes while it appeared he was composing a long text message. But the only words that came though were: Why did you clam up earlier?

Because I couldn't take knowing that you meant those words for Cara and not me. Chanel couldn't admit to that. Instead, she opted for simplicity. A partial truth to lessen the chance of incriminating herself and putting her sister in jeopardy. I was embarrassed.

Again, after a long pause, his response popped up. I meant every word I said.

Why was he being so nice? So sweet? He was such a gentleman that it only served to compound her guilt. When Cara and Chanel had switched places as kids, it had all been in good fun. Harmless. Not like this. Yes, she was protecting her sister, but she was deceiving a father and his child. Chanel wasn't built for this kind of subterfuge.

Christmas couldn't come fast enough. Pulling up the calendar on her phone, Chanel counted forty days until the farce would end. Forty. Let the countdown begin.

Ryder squinted at the large marquee that declared he had arrived at the Divine Hope Fellowship Center. He couldn't remember the last time he had been in an actual church. Gabby's friends at school had invited her to a game night, and their parents had said to dress in casual attire. Though he would have much preferred sitting at home by the fireplace and reading his book on hearing conditions, Ryder had agreed.

Why? Because Gabby needed friends and to socialize.

Ryder pulled in next to Cara's pickup in the church parking lot and curled his hands around the steering wheel. He hadn't expected Cara would be here.

"Are we at the church, Daddy?" Gabby asked in her not-so-quiet whisper.

"Yes…" he said, unbuckling his seat belt and getting out of the car. He felt the sharp sting of the cold evening air and lifted the flap of his jacket to shield his neck from the wind.

Gabby had taken off her pink puffer jacket and knit hat during the short ride. He scrutinized her white wool sweater with a large glitter heart in the center that matched her pink skinny jeans and light-up sneakers.

"Let's get your jacket on," he said.

"I can't wait to see my friends," Gabby said, slipping her hands into the sleeves of her jacket.

"I heard there were going to have burgers." He put

her hat on her head. He wished he had worn his thicker coat over the bomber jacket, but at least they would be inside soon.

"Oh." She wiggled with glee. "I'm going to eat four burgers."

He chuckled. "I don't think so. You'll have a stomach-ache."

Just then, Cara appeared at the door of the church. She wore a long fleece cardigan over a jumpsuit and boots. She must have spotted them, because she waved and scurried toward them. Gabby ran to meet Cara halfway and gave her a big hug.

Ryder locked up his truck and strolled over to where they stood, waiting for him.

"I didn't know you'd be here," Cara said, her cheeks flushed from the cold. "One of the children left the church door open…"

"Gabby was invited by her schoolmates." He had a knot in his stomach, thinking of the crowds, their curiosity and the awkwardness of being the new person in a new place.

"That's great. I wish I had thought to mention it. Every other week, the pastor and youth leader host a youth evening from four to six o'clock. The youth leader had come to my story hour and asked if I would share some stories with the children tonight."

She turned to lead them into the church. Gabby held on to each of their hands.

"I'm cold." Gabby shivered, her teeth chattering. "But I can't wait to see my friends."

Ryder opened the door and allowed Cara and Gabby to go before him, appreciating the blast of warm air. He couldn't wait to get inside. "Yes, it's good to be in the company of friends." He gave Cara a meaningful look.

"Yay!" Gabby bellowed, skipping and jumping when she saw two girls her age race by.

The happiness on Gabby's face stilled any disquiet he felt, and Ryder followed Cara inside. They walked past the sanctuary and into the fellowship hall. There were about fifteen children present, ranging from elementary to high school ages. Several of the tables had games like Checkers, Chutes and Ladders, Twister and Jenga. He could hear a praise song, "The Goodness of God," playing through the overhead speakers, and he smelled burgers and the faint scent of charcoal.

Somebody had braved the weather to grill burgers. His stomach growled, reminding him that he'd skipped lunch, reading books about hearing loss and praying for Gabby.

Gabby had to use the bathroom, so Cara volunteered to take her, leaving Ryder standing near the entrance, uncertain, a hand in his jeans pocket. Just like that, he was taken back to his first days—of high school, of college, on the job—when he had dreaded the discomfort of not knowing anyone in the room.

Then Mrs. Collins walked in, struggling with a forty-eight pack of juices with desserts stacked on top, and his tightened chest eased. He rushed to assist her, taking everything out of her shaky hands.

"Oh, thank you, dear," she said, patting his hand. "Boy, am I glad to see you."

Her warm greeting made him relax even more. In fact, looking around the room, Ryder realized several people were making eye contact, had welcoming smiles and were waving at him. He recognized most of the faces, though he didn't know their names.

The joy of small-town life.

Ryder followed her to the food table and helped or-

ganize the paper goods and napkins. Cara and Gabby
returned, but Gabby didn't come his way. She ran over
to join her friends, who were sorting out the Hi Ho!
Cherry-O boardgame.

Since the food was hot and ready, a man he assumed to be the pastor blessed it, and before Ryder
knew it, he became part of the team serving dinner
to the children—he was on salad. He found he quite
enjoyed helping and was glad no one seemed to mind
his assistance.

Cara and Gabby joined the line. Of course, Gabby
thanked him loudly and asked for no tomatoes with
her salad. Cara winked at him, holding her plate for
him to place a small portion of salad on the side before
moving along.

Once they were finished eating, Cara went up front
and settled into the large chair that had a blanket and a
garland of fall leaves on the back. She read a few books
to a captured audience—Ryder included. The first book
was *Carla and the Christmas Cornbread*. The illus-
trations showed a family in the car heading to spend
time with their grandparents. Seeing the mother driving
with her daughters brought Brittany to mind. His heart
squeezed and he turned a watchful eye on Cara. Her
face held a rapt expression, but she didn't seem upset,
so he released a breath of relief.

Next, Cara read *The Christmas Pumpkin*. As soon
as she turned the page and Gabby saw the pumpkin
patch, his daughter yelled at the top of her lungs, "Me
and Daddy and Ms. Cara went there. We picked pumpkins." Then she jumped to her feet and did a little jig
that made the crowd burst into laughter.

When he moved to try to get her to sit, a few of the
mothers waved at him to let her be, to let her enjoy the

moment. Ryder pulled out his cell phone and captured her on video. On impulse, he turned the camera and recorded Cara for a few minutes. Observing her from behind the lens, he zoomed in, noting her long lashes and those unruly freckles, but he wished he could capture her innate goodness.

Lifting a book high in the air so everyone could see, Cara announced she was going to read *The Giving Snowman*, which was about a snowman who was so helpful that he gave everything he had until he had nothing left. Ryder didn't understand that logic, but his heart squeezed when all whom the snowman had helped then helped him in return. It was an emotional read.

Looking at Gabby, Ryder understood that kind of giving. There wasn't anything he wouldn't do for his little girl. He dabbed at his eyes, swallowing his sudden onslaught of emotion. Of gratitude. This time last year, he hadn't known he had a daughter.

This year, though, his life was full. He had Gabby, and—he looked Cara's way—he had a friend. Life was good.

At the end of the evening, while Gabby was getting a cookie from Mrs. Collins before they departed, Ryder gave Cara a tight hug, holding her a little longer than needed before pulling away.

Giving him a wide smile, Cara asked, "Are you going to bring her again?"

"Most definitely. Gabby had a ball." In fact, he was looking forward to it. "Mrs. Collins told me that the church plans on having a Thanksgiving feast, and I was thinking of coming. What about you?"

Her brown eyes looked…troubled?…for a second, but then she lowered them, shielding him from her thoughts. Her lashes fanned her cheeks. "Yes, I tried to get out of it, but Mrs. Collins can be real persuasive. It's a potluck, so I will probably bring an apple pie from the Amish store or something."

"I'm sure Gabby will be excited to come." And he would treasure spending more time in Cara's presence. "Just promise we'll sit together this time."

"Got it," she said, her smile mysterious.

Cara made a move to leave, but Ryder held her arm. "This might be too much to ask, and I know you'll be busy with your garden, but would you come with me when I take Gabby to see the specialist?"

"Of course," she said, placing a hand on her chest. "I'd be happy to come." Then she touched his chin. "She'll be all right. Believe that. I'll keep you both in my prayers."

His shoulders slumped. "Thank you. I've never been so worried in all my life, so I appreciate your coming." He was amazed at how comfortable he felt sharing his fears with Cara.

"You'll get through it, and I'll be there as much as you need me." Her eyes were filled with compassion, not pity, and her tone held promise.

"I'm going to keep you to your word," he teased to lighten the air.

Cara grew serious, her eyes pleading with him. "No matter what happens in the future, remember that you can depend on me because I value your friendship," she said. "Promise me you'll remember that."

His brows furrowed, but he gave her a nod.

"Good," she said before walking off to help clean up, leaving Ryder to question the caution behind her words.

Dear Reader,

I am writing to announce the launch of a huge **FREE BOOK GIVEAWAY**... and to let you know that YOU are entitled to choose up to FOUR fantastic books that WE pay for.

Try **Love Inspired® Romance Larger-Print** books and fall in love with inspirational romances that take you on an uplifting journey of faith, forgiveness and hope.

Try **Love Inspired® Suspense Larger-Print** books where courage and optimism unite in stories of faith and love in the face of danger.

Or TRY BOTH!

In return, we ask just one favor: Would you please participate in our brief Reader Survey? We'd love to hear from you.

This FREE BOOKS GIVEAWAY means that your introductory shipment is completely free, <u>even the shipping</u>! If you decide to continue, you can look forward to curated monthl shipments of brand-new books from your selected series, always at a discount off the cover price! <u>Plus you can cance any time</u>. Who could pass up a deal like that?

Sincerely

Pam Powers

Pam Powers
For Harlequin Reader Service

Complete the survey below and return it today to receive up to 4 FREE BOOKS and FREE GIFTS guaranteed!

FREE BOOKS GIVEAWAY
Reader Survey

1

Do you prefer books which reflect Christian values?

○ YES ○ NO

2

Do you share your favorite books with friends?

○ YES ○ NO

3

Do you often choose to read instead of watching TV?

○ YES ○ NO

YES! Please send me my Free Rewards, consisting of **2 Free Books from each series I select** and **Free Mystery Gifts**. I understand that I am under no obligation to buy anything, no purchase necessary see terms and conditions for details.

❏ **Love Inspired® Romance Larger-Print** (122/322 IDL GRP7)
❏ **Love Inspired® Suspense Larger-Print** (107/307 IDL GRP7)
❏ **Try Both** (122/322 & 107/307 IDL GRQK)

FIRST NAME	LAST NAME

ADDRESS

APT.#	CITY

STATE/PROV.	ZIP/POSTAL CODE

EMAIL ❏ Please check this box if you would like to receive newsletters and promotional emails from Harlequin Enterprises ULC and its affiliates. You can unsubscribe anytime.

LI/LIS-122-FBG22_LI/LIS-122-FBGVR

Chapter Eleven

During the drive home, Cara's parting words haunted him. He replayed them in his mind, picturing her face, her earnestness, and wondering what that was about. It was almost like Cara was giving him a warning, preparing him for something. He would have mulled on it more if he hadn't heard a light sniffle in the back of the car.

Ryder turned his head briefly to see if Gabby was crying. It was dark in the cab, but he thought he saw her little shoulders shaking.

"Sweetie, what's wrong?" he asked, his eyes furtively searching for a spot where he could pull over if he needed. He was on a back road, and there wasn't a real shoulder, but there was a deserted gas station ahead.

Gabby hiccupped "I—I miss my mommy." At those words, she broke into heart-wrenching sobs.

That story. The Christmas stories must have intensified Gabby's need to connect with Brittany.

Watching out for deer that could dart across the street, Ryder spared her a quick glance. "Oh, honey. I will try to reach her. But you know your mommy loves you, right?"

He swerved into the dark, empty lot, jumped out and

rushed to console her, bending into the truck to rock her in his arms.

"Then why hasn't she called?" Gabby wailed. "Maybe she doesn't care about me anymore."

Ryder's heart broke. Memories of his own abandonment made his anger simmer. No child should question a parent's love. Fighting back his own tears, he said, "Your mother cares. I think she wants to talk to you, but she might not have a signal." He kissed the top of her head. "Mommy is going to call as soon as she can."

"N-no, she won't. She's not going to call," Gabby stammered.

Ryder uttered a prayer for help and lifted his daughter out of the car, tucking her head on his shoulder. He didn't know what to do, but he was stuck in this lot with Gabby, whose tears continued to flow. All he could do was hold her. Hold her until the wave of grief eased.

Besides the night sounds, the area was deserted. He didn't fear for his safety, but it was even colder than it had been before.

A pair of headlights shone in the distance. The vehicle shot past him before coming to a screeching halt. Then he saw the truck back up tentatively into the parking lot, pulling beside his vehicle.

Cara rolled down her window. Her face was illuminated by his parking lights. "Everything all right?"

He didn't need to answer because once Gabby heard Cara's voice, her sobs increased. Her wails echoed through the night. Ryder feared explaining the situation would make Gabby even more upset. Cara shot out of her truck and scurried over to where he stood.

She placed a hand on Gabby's back. "What's wrong, Gabby?" It was so frigid that her breath released small white puffs of air.

"I want my mommy," Gabby said.

Cara's eyes shot to his.

"It's been a while since she's spoken to her," Ryder said.

"Aw…" Cara addressed Gabby, her tone filled with compassion. "I know you miss your mommy, but I have an idea. Do you want to hear what it is?"

Gabby lifted her head, her eyes red, her cheeks puffy and her nose runny. "What?" She sniffled.

"Well, when I'm feeling really sad, I find that praying helps."

Ryder shifted so Gabby had a better angle to talk to Cara. She had stopped crying and was soaking in Cara's words.

"I don't know how to pray," she croaked.

"It's real easy. All you have to do is tell God what's bothering you, what you want. He will listen, and He will answer your prayer."

Gabby cleared her throat and wiped her cheeks. "He will?" she asked, sounding hopeful.

"Yes. God always hears us. I do it all the time, and He helps me feel better every single time."

His stomach clenched. Ryder didn't want Cara telling Gabby that with such certainty. What if Brittany didn't call right away? A few hours seemed like forever to someone Gabby's age, and Ryder knew what it was like to wait for parents who never showed up. Then he berated himself for his lack of faith, pushed back his worry and interjected into the conversation.

"Do you want to pray and ask God to keep mommy safe?" he asked, figuring that would be an easier option.

Tilting her head, Gabby placed a finger on her lips like she was thinking. He waited a few tense seconds before she said, "Yes."

"Great. Well, let's go in Daddy's truck since it is much warmer in there, and then you can pray," Cara said.

"I want to pray. I want to ask God to let my mommy call."

Fresh doubts arose, his faith plummeting to his boots. Ryder wished Gabby would pray for her mother's safety. It was a little more abstract. Something specific like calling…that might lead to more tears and disappointment.

Cara, on the other hand, didn't seem to have any second thoughts. With a nod, she strode over with confidence and opened the passenger door. Swallowing his reservations, Ryder put Gabby in the back and got in his car.

He rubbed his hands and turned up the fan so heat could circulate. Then Ryder turned on the interior lights and reached over to search the glove box for napkins.

"Wipe your face," he said gently, handing one to Gabby.

Ryder gave his daughter a reassuring smile and tried to look serene, but on the inside, he was praying, *Please, God, answer her prayer. Please let Brittany call.*

Unaware of his turmoil, Cara twisted in her seat and addressed Gabby. "Are you ready to pray?"

Gabby nodded.

Cara took charge and Ryder was relieved because doubt had squeezed its fist, tightening his voice box.

"Okay, clasp your hands and close your eyes."

Gabby did as she said, making Ryder's heart melt. His eyes felt glassy.

"Great," Cara said. "Now, start with, 'Dear God,' and ask Him for whatever you want."

As if sensing his nervousness, Cara gave his hand a squeeze and whispered, "Trust God."

Gabby began to pray. Cara closed her eyes, but Ryder kept his gaze pinned on Gabby.

"Dear God, I miss my mommy so much. She doesn't know I lost my tooth, and I want to tell her that I was brave. Can you please, please have my mommy call, because it's going to be Christmas soon and I—" Her voice little cracked, piercing Ryder's heart. "I need to know she's okay." She opened her eyes. "What do I do now?"

Cara dabbed at her eyes. "Just say, 'In Jesus's name, Amen.'"

Gabby repeated the words. When she was done, all three of them needed new napkins. Cara was visibly shaken, blowing her nose. Ryder wiped his cheeks before reaching over, intending to help Gabby.

Though her eyes were filled with tears, she had a big smile on her face. His brows shot up his forehead. "Are you okay?" he asked.

"Yes. I feel good because I know God is going to answer me." She sniffled and swung her legs. "Can we go home? I don't want to miss my mommy's call."

He marveled at her innocent faith, stronger than his, and slid a worried glance Cara's way, his shoulders tense.

Giving him a tender smile, Cara mouthed, "Have faith," before leaving him to deal with Gabby and a potential crying fest if the cell phone didn't play the incoming-call melody.

Chanel needed a double portion of the same faith she'd told Ryder to have. As soon as she entered her house, she dashed up the stairs and into her prayer closet. Hearing Gabby pray with such certainty moved her. When God's Word said we should be like chil-

dren, that was what He meant. She intended to pray
the same request for Cara to call. The text had said she
was okay, but Chanel didn't know how badly her sister had been hurt.

That worry churned nonstop.

Falling to her knees, she rested her elbows on the
prayer bench and began to pray for God's protection for
her sister and for the Frost family. She ended the prayer
asking God to have both women reach out.

Once she was done, Chanel decided not to fret on
when God would answer. She knew He was going to
come through, and for the first time in years, she made
up her mind to walk in that belief.

Exactly nineteen minutes later, Chanel's FaceTime
went off. It was Cara. All Chanel could do was utter a
word of praise. Her hands shook, so she had to grip the
phone with both hands to keep it steady.

"Sis, you called. You called." Chanel released her
tears. "Are you all right?" She tried to gauge her sister's whereabouts based on the background, but all she
saw was a white wall.

"Yes," Cara said, blurring the background. "I, uh, I
got shot. A bullet grazed my right leg." *Grazed.*

"Wh-what happened?" Her heart pumped at a furious rhythm in her chest. Chanel's legs weakened, and
she went to sit on the edge of her bed. She had good
reception, but there was a second modem in her bedroom, and she wasn't chancing losing this call due to
poor connection. Even though her sister was alive to
talk about it, she was now feeling the aftereffects of
knowing Cara could have been killed.

"You're not going to believe this," her sister said,
shaking her head, "but it was an accident. Me and the

agent received a tip on Jeremiah's location, and we were staking out the area. I can't go into all the details, but the FBI agent fired a shot that ricocheted and hit me instead of Jeremiah. That gave him the opportunity to get away."

"Wow." Chanel touched her chest, her eyes going wide. "How on earth could that have happened? I thought FBI agents were trained better than that."

"Chanel, look at me," Cara said, her voice firm. "It was an accident and comes with the territory of a job like this one. Wearing any kind of badge leaves you at risk for getting in harm's way. He already feels horrible, so let it go. It was a mistake."

Chanel's eyes narrowed. "You're defending the man that shot you?" That was so unlike her sister. Cara was unforgiving when it came to any kind of mistake.

"I'm learning that being human means there is a chance for imperfection, no matter how careful or perfect the plan."

"I'm impressed. That FBI agent must be something else to gain your respect." Or something more? She thought it but wouldn't voice that aloud. If there was something to tell, Cara would tell her when she was ready. Cocking her head, Chantel asked, "Does that mean you forgive yourself for Jeremiah's escape?"

Cara couldn't meet her eyes. She fiddled with her black jacket. "I'm coming to terms with it."

"Good, because you didn't tell me that you were helping a pregnant woman when that happened. I had to hear about it and then read about it to know all the details."

"I know—but at the time, all I could think about was

how a murderer was still on the loose, and I had let him go under my watch."

Chanel rolled her eyes. "Take your own advice and chalk it up to the job. You saved a baby's life. I think you did the right thing, sis. Because if I could have saved my—" She cut off, unable to continue, and cleared her throat. "You did the right thing."

"Okay." Cara looked at her watch. "I only have a few minutes, but how are things with Ryder and that mutt of his?"

"Wolf isn't a mutt," she huffed out. "He's wonderful, and Ryder is…my friend."

Cara's eyebrow arched. "Friend?" She gave her twin a knowing glance.

"You sure you'll be home by Christmas?" Chanel asked, deflecting from having to talk about Ryder. She didn't know how she felt.

"Yes, I should be." She looked behind her and then at her watch. Chanel knew that meant she only had seconds left with her sister.

"I'll be praying to that end." Chanel's voice broke. "Please be careful. I love you."

"I love you too." And with that, she was gone.

Chanel inhaled and exhaled several times. Since she had gotten a call, Chanel had to text to find out if Gabby's mother had called. Has Gabby spoken to her mom?

His response was almost immediate. No. She hasn't called.

How's Gabby?

Good, so far. Hopefully, we will hear from her tomorrow.

Stay positive.

A thumbs-up emoji was his final response. She rested her cell phone next to her on the bed, her thoughts returning to Cara.

Her sister was safe, and she could be home by Christmas, which was wonderful because that was their favorite holiday. Well, it was mostly Chanel's. Cara was more like the Grinch, who had to be coerced into having a good time, but at least they'd be together. She walked around their family home. Her sister had taken care of the property, but some things were in need of refurbishing. Refreshing. Chanel wanted to give the house a face-lift to get it Christmas ready. It would take a considerable amount of funds...

Biting her lower lip, Chanel thought of Warren's insurance payout that had remained untouched, accumulating interest for fifteen years. Maybe it was time she dipped into it to restore the farm and the house. Her stomach clenched. Warren would have wanted that.

But she didn't know if she could bring herself to touch the money he had to die for her to receive. She had left it in the bank in defiance of his death, as if not claiming it would assuage her guilt. But it hadn't. The guilt grew and festered into a dump pile she didn't have the strength to remove.

Shaking her head like she was shaking off the idea, Chanel strolled into the kitchen to put on the teakettle to make a cup of peppermint tea.

Turning on the back-porch light, Chanel wandered outside and looked over at the vegetable garden. The bags of soil and garden supplies she had purchased were in the same spot, untouched. She hadn't even begun to expand the garden.

Yet.

She hadn't begun to do it *yet*. And Ryder had offered to help…

No. She had to stop depending on and thinking about Ryder so much. She needed to tackle the yard on her own or hire a company if she couldn't do it. But she wouldn't ask Ryder Frost for help. Their lives were becoming too intertwined, too interdependent, even if they were friends.

Thinking about Warren was a harsh reminder that Chanel needed to keep her emotional distance.

The teakettle whistled on cue, like it was sending an alarm signal to her brain. She would keep the boundaries between herself and Ryder very clear. No matter how thoughtful he was, or how sweet Gabby was, they were not her family. She mustn't get too involved, care too much—what would she do if she lost them?

Chanel went to still the kettle's fury, mindful of the steam. If she got too close—to the steam or the Frosts—she could get a third-degree burn. She couldn't risk getting burned a second time, because that was a pain from which she might never recover.

Chapter Twelve

God was giving him a spiritual workout. For two days—forty-eight hours—he sweated while he waited, all the while marveling at Gabby's mustard-seed faith. His little princess never stopped smiling. Instead, she would ask in the morning and evenings if Ryder had heard from her mom, and he would tense when he told her that he hadn't, expecting Gabby to fall apart.

But she only tilted her head and said, "God's going to do it. Because I asked Him."

Every time she said that, her quiet confidence punched him in the gut. Ryder could only nod and say, "Yep. He will."

On the evening of the second day, Gabby sat at the kitchen table with her legs tucked under her. She was coloring in her Disney-princess coloring book when she made the usual inquiry about her mother calling, and he gave his typical response. But this time, she narrowed her gaze and looked at him like she was seeing his thoughts. "Do you believe that she's going to call, Daddy?"

He stepped back. "Um. Well, she might be busy."

Gabby's face fell. Picking up her crayon, she said,

"That's why she hasn't yet. Because you don't believe it's impawsible."

"You mean *possible*." His mouth popped open at her perceptiveness. She was five, but her thinking was that of someone twenty years older. "Of course I think it's possible." It was only logical that Brittany would reach out eventually.

"But you have to belief," she insisted, getting to her feet and walking over to him.

"I do *believe*," he replied, putting emphasis on the word.

"Then, can you pray, Daddy?" she asked, putting a hand on her hip like she was grown.

I have been praying, he wanted to say. But had he really prayed with the kind of faith required? "Okay, honey, I will pray."

He held her hand and prayed to God to ask that He allow Brittany to call. As soon as he ended the prayer and Gabby had returned to her coloring, his cell phone rang. Hope filled his chest when he looked at the screen. But it was a number he had identified as spam. Defeated, he allowed the call to go to voice mail. He slipped the phone in his back pocket and exhaled, feeling silly for thinking God would come through that fast.

Did God view his prayers as spam calls? A nuisance? An annoyance? A disturbance compared to even more important prayers?

He squelched those questions and recited Matthew 7:9 under his breath. "Or what man is there of you, whom if his son ask bread, will he give him a stone?" God wouldn't do that, and he would keep repeating the Scripture until it became his truth.

Later that night, after he had tucked in Gabby and gotten into his king-size bed, his cell phone rang. It was facedown on his nightstand, and Ryder almost let the call go to voice mail. Almost.

The mustard-seed hope refused to die.

Even though his eyes burned, Ryder picked up the phone, yawned and uttered a sleepy, "Hello?"

"Ryder?" the voice asked.

"Brittany? Is that you?" He shot up, wide awake, and threw off the covers. "Of course it's you."

"I'm so glad I finally got through," she said, laughing and sounding relieved. "You don't know how many times I tried to reach you, but I couldn't get a signal."

"It's okay. It's okay. We prayed. Gabby prayed for you to call."

"Well, He must have heard your prayers, because this is the first clear line I have gotten in weeks."

He put her on speaker, scampered into Gabby's room and turned on the light. Then he gave his daughter a light shake. "Gabby, wake up, wake up. Mommy's on the phone."

She sat up with his help, her head lolling from side to side, and rubbed her eyes. "What?"

"It's Mommy, sweetie. Mommy is on the phone."

"Oh." Her voice sounded groggy and lacked enthusiasm—a sure sign that Gabby was not awake enough for his words to register.

"Gabby?" Brittany called out, but Gabby's eyes remained closed. Ryder had to prop her up with his elbow to keep her from falling back onto her pillow. Great. God had answered her prayer, but she was too tired to know.

He slipped to his knees by the edge of her bed, wiped his brow and tried again, his voice in a panic. Ryder wasn't sure how long Brittany would be able to stay on the call or when she would be able to call again, so it was imperative Gabby talk to her mother now.

"Gabby. Gabby. Mommy is on the phone. You've got to wake up."

"Gabby, baby, it's Mommy," Brittany said in a louder tone. He could hear the slight hysteria in her voice and knew that Brittany also feared disconnection.

Lord, please let Gabby wake up.

One little eye popped open. "Mommy?"

"Yes, honey," he said, relieved. "You wanted to talk to Mommy, and God answered your prayer."

She emitted a loud yawn and opened her other eye, seeming more alert. "Mommy, I asked God for you to call me, and He did it."

"I'm so glad you did," Brittany said. "Ryder, can you hold up the phone so I can see her?"

She was on FaceTime? He must have been sleepier than he thought. Ryder held the device up in Gabby's line of vision.

"Oh, baby, I see you. I see you." Brittany began to cry. "I miss you so much."

"I miss you too. Guess what, Mommy. Guess what! I lost my tooth!" she yelled.

Taking the phone from him, Gabby began to pace the room just like Ryder did when he was on the phone. Ryder's lip quirked. He sat on the carpet, scooting until his back was against the wall while his daughter filled Brittany in on everything she could remember. Gabby mentioned Cara's name several times.

Ryder knew Brittany would be asking him about her once Gabby was off the phone.

"Are you coming home for Christmas?" Gabby asked. He waited with bated breath for Brittany's response.

"Um… I'll see, baby," Brittany said.

Uh-oh. He knew that meant Brittany wouldn't be back by Christmas and was stalling, unsure of how to tell Gabby.

"You said we would have a real Christmas this time," Gabby said, clutching the phone. Her face crumpled like she was about to cry.

"Uh, something came up. But I mailed you a present. It should get there way before Christmas."

"But it's not the same," Gabby said, her voice breaking. She came over to where Ryder sat and dropped onto his lap. Gabby hid her face in his chest, holding the phone away from her.

Ryder had to clamp his jaw shut to keep from interfering. Instead, he wrapped his arms around Gabby and urged her to talk to her mother. She did, but her voice lacked excitement. Her body slumped against his, feeling as weighty as her disappointment.

"Let me talk to Daddy," Brittany finally said when she couldn't appease Gabby anymore. "I love you, Gabby."

"I love you too," Gabby said, handing Ryder the phone and running back into her bed. She covered her head and burrowed under the covers. He could hear her quiet sobs, but he knew he had to talk with Brittany in private before he could console his child.

"You know she's disappointed, right?" he said, furious that Brittany wasn't keeping her word.

Her large eyes pleaded with him. "I got a chance to take part in this groundbreaking research, and they won't let me take Gabby. Can you explain that to her for me?"

"You expect a five-year-old to understand why her mother can't be here for Christmas? Why can't you take a break?"

"Not everyone in the world celebrates Christmas, and I have the chance to become the lead. The flights are too expensive, and I'd spend most of the couple days I have off traveling. Gabby and I can have Christmas when I return," Brittany said, her voice steely. "She knows my work is important—"

"More important than her?" he challenged. Bitterness rose within him. His parents had put his feelings last, and to see the same thing happen to Gabby stoked his fury.

"I had Gabby for five years, toting her along with me. I just can't take her on these expeditions. Besides, I can't concentrate with her here."

His chest heaved and he told himself not to judge Brittany by his parents' actions. "I get it. But don't you see how this is hurting her?" This punctured him deep in his core. "I love that little girl with everything within me, and she needs you." He stopped and exhaled long plumes of air, trying to calm himself. He wasn't going to beg a mother to spend time with her child. He wasn't.

"I'm sorry," she said, her tone repentant.

He ran a hand through his hair and rubbed his temples. "The milk is already spilled, so to speak." Changing topics, he asked, "When are you coming back?"

"Right after New Year's."

He nodded. Gabby was going to be upset, but he would have more time with his daughter. "Did you get my emails about sending all her medical records and that Gabby has to see an ear specialist?"

"Yes, I did," she said, her tone now calmer and businesslike. "I emailed you scanned copies right before I called. The originals are packed in the box with Gabby's Christmas present." Brittany leaned closer to the camera. "Care to tell me about Cara?"

Ryder didn't miss the fact that she hadn't asked about Gabby's referral to the specialist. She was more concerned about his next-door neighbor.

"She's a friend." That's all he would say. He gave her a challenging look, hoping Brittany didn't have a problem with Cara being in Gabby's life. Because Gabby would be devastated.

After a few beats, Brittany said, "I see. I trust you, and Gabby seems to like her—so I'm fine with it, I guess."

He could hear the jealousy in her tone and knew it was about Gabby. Ryder rushed to reassure her. "No one can take your place, Brittany. You're her mother. Remember that."

"I know," she said, wiping the corner of her eye. "I just needed to hear you say that." Her lower lip quivered. "I don't want Gabby to hate me."

"She doesn't. She loves you. So don't worry about that. You didn't desert her. You left her with me. Her father. The past few months with Gabby here have added meaning to my life in ways that I can't explain. I would have her for a lifetime if I could. If you wanted me to." There, he had said it. Planted a seed. Maybe it would develop into something.

"Gabby is a precious little girl," Brittany said, straightening. "But I am coming back for her."

"Okay," he said. "But we can work out something once you're back in the States, because I need my daughter in my life. Maybe we can get joint custody."

She averted her eyes. "I've got to go, but please email me and let me know what's going on with her hearing," Brittany said before she disconnected the video call.

Ryder went to check on Gabby. His daughter was

sound asleep. He turned off her bedroom light and closed her door before traipsing down the stairs.

Wolf's ears perked up, and he gave a little moan.

It was late. Really late. But Ryder couldn't get to sleep until he reached out to Cara. She would want to know that they had finally heard from Gabby's mom.

He sent her a quick text. Prayers have been answered.

She replied so fast that Ryder knew she had to have already been awake. Woot! Woot!

Sauntering over to look out his living room window, he could see her bedroom light was on. Want to fill you in. Meet me outside in five?

The three dots danced until her answer appeared. I'm bringing hot chocolate.

"Ms. Cara's coming over," Ryder said to Wolf, opening the front door.

At that, his dog stood and shook his fur. Then he joined Ryder by the door, wagging his tail. Wolf appeared to be as anxious to see her as he.

Chanel didn't cry over spilled paint. She kicked the can instead. Okay, it had been an unintentional accident, and the can had been on tarp, but the end result was that her wooden floor had been marred with paint the size of teardrops. She had been cleaning paint off her kitchen floor when Ryder's text came through. So she was more than ready for a break.

After tossing her soiled pants and work boots into the trash, she changed into a dark blue track suit and sneakers and donned a thick coat before hiking across the yard to Ryder's house. She held a thermos of hot cocoa she had quickly mixed up. Maybe it was the hour, but Chanel hadn't thought to ask Ryder to make the hot cocoa since she was going to his house and not the other way around.

Wolf yelped when he saw her. She gave the hand signal for him to sit. When he did, Ryder clapped. "He's come so far."

"I think we will have our last lesson tomorrow morning, and then I'll let Wolf show off his skills."

"I don't know how I can thank you," Ryder said.

She thought about the paint on her kitchen floor. "I do." She explained the dilemma.

Ryder laughed. "I'll bring a can of acetone when I come over tomorrow morning. That should do the trick, and your floors should be good as new. Oh, don't forget that we're going to Gabby's appointment at twelve thirty."

"I have it marked on my calendar," Chanel said. She was glad he had asked her to tag along, because she would have texted him every five minutes to ask what was going on anyway.

She held up the thermos, and he went to the kitchen cabinets to get two big mugs. Returning outside, handed them to her, and she poured cocoa for each of them. Handing him one of the steaming mugs, she curled her fingers around the other, welcoming the warmth against her hand. Blowing on it, Chanel sat in one of the chairs on Ryder's porch and took a sip. Wolf settled by her, using her leg as a back scratcher.

"So, what happened with Gabby's mom?" she asked, not bothering to hide her curiosity. She was eager to know more about the woman who had given birth to such a sweet child and captured Ryder's interest, even if for a short time.

"Gabby was excited to finally hear from her. Brittany is in some remote location, so it was hard for her to reach us, but she's sending over Gabby's pertinent information along with her Christmas gift."

Chanel furrowed her brows. "I thought she was coming in time for Christmas?"

"Her plans changed. She won't be back until after New Year's. Or at least, that's what she said." His tone implied that he didn't believe her. Ryder gave a little chuckle. "I even brought up the idea of joint custody, though what I really wanted to say is that she should just leave Gabby here with me full-time and visit when she pleases." He sat in a chair next to her, drank some of his hot chocolate and rested his mug on the floor. "I know she wouldn't do that, though."

Chanel heard the secret yearning in his voice and wished there was an easy solution. "How did Gabby take it when she heard her mother wasn't coming home in time for Christmas?"

"She was upset. When Brittany was leaving, she promised to give Gabby a spectacular Christmas, since Gabby's never had a chance to really celebrate the holiday. She was always on some excavation site with her mother, so any celebration had to be minor."

"Oh, wow." Her chest constricted. "Every child deserves to have a memorable Christmas. Besides honoring Christ, Christmas is all about spending time with family and opening presents first thing in the morning. I remember not being able to sleep the night before because I couldn't wait to see what my parents had gotten me."

And her sister. Chanel and Cara had often received similar presents in different colors. But she couldn't mention that. She felt a pang at having to leave that out. Every year for the past forty-one years, Cara and Chanel had spent the holiday together. Of course, Cara had traveled to Chanel's house since she wouldn't come here.

Except this year.

She looked over at Ryder, who had gone quiet. He was staring straight ahead, sipping his hot chocolate.

To distract herself, she continued, "Although, as I got older, the best part was stringing the popcorn, making eggnog and watching *It's a Wonderful Life*. It's sort of a family tradition."

Her neighbor didn't say a word.

"What about you?" she asked, thinking she had been rambling so much that he hadn't had a chance to contribute to the conversation. "What do you remember most about Christmas?"

"My parents leaving me."

His words made her gasp. She slapped her forehead. "Oh, Ryder. I was so caught up… It slipped my mind…"

"No. It's okay." He turned to face her. "I haven't celebrated Christmas since that day. For me, it's just another day, so I didn't mind that Brittany was coming for Gabby, because then I wouldn't have to worry about it. But now that she isn't coming, I don't know what I'm going to do. I don't have any good memories about December twenty-fifth."

She held her stomach. Hearing the sorrow in Ryder's voice made her heart ache. "How about we get through Thanksgiving? It's not even December yet, so you'll have quite a few weeks to get used to the idea."

"I don't have to get used to something I don't do."

His tone sounded final.

Even though her mind told her to let the matter rest, Chanel couldn't remain quiet. "I'm sorry, but you're a parent now. This isn't about you. It's about Gabby and what she needs."

Ryder's lips curled. "She doesn't need a holiday to know I love her. I tell her that every day," he said, his tone frostier than the night air. "I think you have a different definition of *need* than I do. Gabby needs clothes, food and shelter, and I have provided that for her," he said, pointing toward the house. "That's what she needs."

Putting a hand over her mouth, Chanel said, "I didn't mean to suggest—"

"Oh yes, you did," Ryder said, cutting her off. "You're not a parent. So don't presume to try to tell me what to do with my child."

She sucked in a huge breath. Her mug crashed to the floor. Chanel didn't realize she'd loosened her hand to touch her chest. His harsh words sliced her to the core, and for a moment, she felt as if she couldn't breathe.

Looking at Ryder, Chanel couldn't believe he had said those words knowing how much she had wanted children.

Standing, Chanel rushed down the steps, almost tripping in her haste to get home.

She felt a hand on her back and flinched.

Ryder spun her around to face him. His eyes were wide, like he himself was having trouble processing what he had said. He touched her cheek, "Oh, Cara. I was upset. I didn't mean that."

Her eyes filled. "But you said it. And words, once spoken, cannot be taken back or forgotten."

Chapter Thirteen

"Good job, Wolf," Chanel said at the end of their obedience-training lesson. Ryder had sent Wolf over without him. A smart move on his part. After running the dog through several commands, Chanel knew Wolf was ready to graduate. She wrapped her arms around the animal's neck and kissed his fur. Then she signaled for him to sit while she went into the house.

Carefully, she made her way outside, giggling at Wolf's tongue hanging out of his mouth.

"You just know you're the best, now, don't you? Well, let's see how you do when Ryder and Gabby get here."

She had sent Ryder a text asking him to come over with Gabby. It was the only text she had sent, ignoring the many she'd received from him the night before and through the morning, apologizing. Every time he said he was sorry, he followed it up with a long explanation.

For most of the night, Chanel hadn't slept, soaking the pillow with her tears. When she awakened, her eyes were beet red, her nose stuffy and she'd had a massive headache. She'd taken an aspirin, slapped sunglasses on and went outside to face the day.

And she'd decided that she would still go with them

to the ear specialist, for Gabby's sake, since one of Ryder's numerous messages had emphasized that he wanted her to go. She was upset with him, but Chanel knew he would need her support.

At exactly 10:19 a.m., Ryder and Gabby stepped outside his house. He looked over at her and gave a little wave. Chanel wouldn't have returned it if she hadn't seen Gabby waving as well, hollering out Cara's name. Then they headed her way, walking across the lawn, hand in hand. Chanel could see he was carrying a small can—probably the acetone.

Twisting out of her father's grip, Gabby dashed across the yard and hurled herself into Chanel's arms. She closed her eyes, inhaling the scent of apples and cinnamon. Gabby's hair was in a high bun that rested against Chanel's cheek. Ryder had placed little butterfly clips on different parts of the bun. She had on a lighter jacket since it wasn't as cold as the day before. In fact, the expected temperature for the day was close to sixty-four degrees. That was Delaware weather, though. Chanel squeezed both of Gabby's shoulders before releasing her.

To her surprise, Gabby kissed her on the cheek. Her cold little lips left not only an imprint on Chanel's face but also her heart. Gabby was burrowing her way past Chanel's defenses and becoming harder and harder to resist.

"Hey," Ryder said, standing hesitantly at the foot of the steps. He pulled his jacket closer to his chest. Since she was wearing sunglasses, Chanel felt free to check him out. He looked slightly ragged, like he hadn't slept much, and had a five-o'clock shadow. *Good.* If he'd appeared well rested, she would have been surprised.

"Have a seat," she said, gesturing to the chairs. He

handed off the can of acetone and slipped into one of the chairs at the glass table.

Signaling to Wolf, Chanel had the dog demonstrate all he had learned. The pup responded to her voice commands and hand gestures.

Each time the dog completed a task, Gabby bellowed, "Go, Wolf! You got this!"

Chanel couldn't stop herself from grinning at the little girl's enthusiasm.

Then Chanel had Ryder stand with her. Keeping her tone noncommittal and professional, she tutored him through all the commands until Ryder was comfortable doing them on his own. Once they were finished, Chanel had Gabby practice using the same commands with Wolf. At the end of their session, Gabby took Wolf on the lawn to play, giving Chanel and Ryder a chance to talk.

"Thank you so much, Cara," he said. "I wish you would allow me to pay you. Wolf is a completely different dog."

"It's all good," she said. "I'm not about to charge my friend."

His brow arched. "Am I your friend?"

"Yes." She nodded. "Despite how you lashed out at me, I consider you a friend."

"I'm sorry." This time he kept the apology heartfelt and simple.

"Don't do it again," she said, her voice stern. "Don't slap the hand that's trying to help you."

Cara's forgiving nature amazed him. Ryder hadn't expected her to end their spat so quickly. He had been prepared to seek her forgiveness for days. Instead, she had given him another chance.

One that he valued and respected.

Once he had sent Wolf inside and secured the doggy door, Ryder, Cara and Gabby drove to the ear specialist in New Castle County. Now they sat huddled together, with Gabby on Cara's lap, waiting on the doctor to enter the room with the results.

For some reason, Cara seemed on edge. She had wanted to wait in the car and then the reception area, but Ryder wasn't having that. She kept fiddling with the hair by her left ear.

Dr. Simpson came in, holding a chart and X-rays in her hand. She was average height and had thick, round glasses, but her eyes were sharp and her handshake firm. The doctor pointed to the corner of the room that had a small library where Gabby could check out the picture books while she addressed them.

"I took a moment to review her medical history and her scans." Her eyes darted back and forth between them. "I concur with Dr. Wallen's findings. Your daughter does have moderate-to-severe hearing loss in both ears. The audiology exam showed that sound vibrations are not reaching her inner ear or cochlea."

"Do you know what caused it?" Ryder asked. "Was it congenital?"

Pushing her glasses up the bridge of her nose, Dr. Simpson said, "In reviewing your daughter's file, Gabby suffers from chronic ear infections. Left untreated, they can lead to hearing loss. In Gabby's case, she was given medications to treat her ear infections, so we will seek an alternate cure."

"Does this mean she will have to get hearing aids?" he asked. Since the medications hadn't worked, that was the next least-invasive procedure.

The doctor shook her head. "I'm actually recommending cochlear implants to improve her hearing and ear tubes to take care of the infections. It's a one-day surgery with recovery at home."

Ryder's heart froze at the word *surgery*, though he had done the research and knew that was a possibility. Research wasn't reality. And the reality was that, though he was a scientist, Ryder was also a father. This father didn't like the thought of his daughter even needing a Band-Aid, much less going through any kind of medical procedure.

"What's the difference between hearing aids and implants?" Cara asked with a light tremor in her tone.

Though she wasn't the biological parent, her concern for Gabby was obvious, making him feeling guiltier for the words he'd tossed at her in anger.

"Hearing aids are for mild-to-moderate hearing loss. Cochlear implants are best for more severe loss and for those with structural damage to the ear." The doctor's eyes narrowed and she tilted her head. "I'm sorry, but do I know you? You look familiar. I never forget a face."

Cara shook her head and fussed with her jacket. "No, uh, I… You might have me confused with someone else."

Dr. Simpson scrutinized her keenly. "I'm positive I know you. It will come back to me."

"No. You must have me mixed up with someone else," Cara said. She sounded out of breath, like she was nervous.

"Oh, okay… If you say so." The doctor excused herself to get Ryder some informational pamphlets.

Ryder looked over at Cara, whose face had paled. He touched her arm. "Are you okay?"

She stood up and tapped her feet. "Yeah, I, uh, need to get some air."

Ryder didn't understand what had just happened, but as Cara left, Dr. Simpson returned, holding several flyers. "I have some reading material that covers what to expect during cochlear implant surgery and recovery. You'll need to schedule the surgery for after the holidays, as I'm booked until mid-December."

That meant Gabby wouldn't be able to leave right after New Year's. She would need to stay with him a little longer. That was the only benefit he saw.

With that, Dr. Simpson escorted him and Gabby to the reception area. With Ryder's permission, the assistant at the front desk gave Gabby a lollipop and a sticker. From the corner of his eye, he saw Cara pacing outside the building as he made the appointment. He was given the second week in January. Tucking the appointment card into his pocket, Ryder led Gabby out of the office.

He would email Brittany to update her and to let her know the doctor's recommendation. She wouldn't object.

In her last email with Gabby's personal documents, she had mentioned some excursion for which she was writing a grant. As if she was preparing him. Ryder anticipated Brittany would soon ask for another extension on Gabby's stay with him. The researcher's life was like a black hole: it could suck you in on so many paths that you could keep digging for truths, for the next scientific discovery, indefinitely, forgetting about those most important in your life. For many, if given an ultimatum, they would choose research.

Not Ryder.

He chose Gabby. And he would choose her always. For life.

Chapter Fourteen

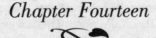

Chanel finished putting the last tablecloth on the huge round table in the fellowship hall. After they had feasted, the congregation would gather in the sanctuary for an evening of praise instead of partaking in the Black Friday rush.

She had volunteered, along with two other members, to help with the Thanksgiving Day decorations and to put up the huge Christmas tree in the corner of the room where all the children would make and add their own ornaments. She had added her store bought pie to the potluck. Thanksgiving dinner was not the time for poor cooks like herself to experiment. It was a time to showcase your main dish.

Everybody knew Mrs. Collins would bring her famous peach cobbler; she had won awards for it at the county fair. Mr. Mullings would bring fried turkeys, and Sister Henry had to do the mac and cheese. In fact, the sign-up sheet was just for show. It was already known who was bringing what, and in the fifteen years since she had last been to Hawk's Landing, that hadn't changed.

She had seen the same familiar names on the paper

pinned to the announcement board. However, Chanel did recognize a new one. Ryder had scrawled his name to bring coleslaw. All she knew was it had better be on point or the town would never forget. Never.

The one time she had dared to make cookies—*cookies*—and burned the bottoms, she had been dubbed Cookie Monstress for years. If she remembered right, someone had even made her a T-shirt with the name imprinted on it. Hopefully, none of the townspeople would mention "Chanel" in Ryder's hearing. She doubted they would, because she hadn't been to town in years.

Her heart constricted. It was sad that when she did come back, it was to pretend to be Cara.

Thinking of Cara, Chanel whispered, "I hope you're enjoying today, wherever you are. And staying safe."

Gathering the plates, glasses and utensils, she began to dress the tables. The other volunteer took care of the table accessories. Each table had large round candles with gold accents, orange cloth napkins and small bonsai trees.

Gold and orange streamers ran across the ceiling, and a balloon garland was placed in one of the corners of the room. The pastor—Divine Hope's unofficial deejay— was in the back of the room, setting up his equipment.

Just as she had finished, Ryder and Gabby entered the hall with a large group of people. He looked handsome in his gray sweater and black slacks. Gabby had on a long-sleeved shirt with a tutu, white stockings and black Mary Janes. Her hair had been done like Princess Leia of *Star Wars*.

"You look so adorable, Gabby," Chanel said.

"Thank you. May the fart be with you," she said with gusto, loud enough to get a few gasps, and then curtsied.

Chanel covered her mouth to hide her grin.

"No. It's *force. Force.*" Ryder sighed, his consternation evident. "You don't know how many times we practiced that line."

"I keep messing up," Gabby said, leaning into her father's leg. She peered up at Chanel from under her lashes, and Chanel's heart expanded. Gabby was hard to keep out. With every contact, Chanel's resolve weakened. The little girl was like a blowtorch, melting every single resistance surrounding Chanel's heart.

"Where did you put the coleslaw?" she asked.

"Mrs. Collins took it from me," he said, surveying the space. "Did you work on the seating arrangements?"

"No. You can pretty much sit where you want."

"I want to sit over there," Gabby interjected, pointing to a table designated for children.

"That's fine," Ryder said, then turned his baby blues Chanel's way and lowered his voice. "And I want to sit with you."

Chanel chose a table near the rear. If her heart rate accelerated at his words, she would ignore it. He sat to the left of her and scooted close. She got a whiff of his cologne, which seemed to be a combination of sage and woods, and her nose definitely approved.

"You look lovely. The dress brings out the color of your eyes."

Lowering her head so her hair could hide her blush, she whispered a shy, "Thank you. You don't look too bad yourself." Chanel had chosen a formfitting pumpkin-colored sweater dress paired with brown boots. She wore a pearl necklace that had belonged to her mother and gold earrings that were Cara's, and she had kept her makeup light.

Glancing around the room, Chanel could see quite a few more people had arrived and were choosing their seats. The pastor had gotten the music started, and the air felt festive. Chanel's stomach sang to the aroma of the food. Quite loudly, in fact.

"Someone's hungry," Ryder teased.

"I only had a cup of coffee," she said. "I had to leave room in my tummy for this goodness." She bopped her head to a catchy praise tune she had never heard before.

"We had a light breakfast, so I am definitely ready to eat." Ryder dipped close to her left ear. "I'm glad you—"

Her hearing aid beeped. Oh, no. Her battery must be low, and Ryder was talking steadily. Chanel wished she'd had him sit on her right side. Starting to hyperventilate, she jumped to her feet.

"Are you okay?" Ryder asked. He stood as well and touched her shoulder, peering into her eyes.

"I—I'll be right back," she said, grabbing her bag and scurrying toward the restroom. She hoped she had brought her spare batteries, or this could be the end of the charade. She darted into the stall meant for the disabled because it had a mirror and would give her some privacy.

Closing the door behind her, she rested both hands on either side of the sink and drew deep breaths. This was all too much. She didn't know how much longer she would be able to manage this double life.

First, she was lying to Ryder. Lying every day. Then he had made Gabby's appointment with the same specialist she'd had fifteen years ago when she lost most of her hearing after the boat accident. What were the odds it would be the same doctor? She wished she had asked where they were going and who Gabby would be seeing, but Chanel hadn't thought it would be the same physician after all those years.

It had taken all her willpower to pretend not to remember Dr. Simpson. Especially since the doctor had been adamant about knowing her. She probably had a photographic memory. Chanel hadn't been able to stay in the room because of her conscience, so she'd run out of the building before the end of the appointment. She had been relieved when Ryder hadn't questioned her quick exit.

She needed to tell Ryder the truth. Truth was like a seed: there was no burying it for long. It sprouted and grew and revealed itself in time. She clutched her chest. Chanel knew time was not on her side. If—no, *when*—she was exposed as Cara's twin and she hadn't been the one to tell him, Ryder would be hurt. Well, he would be hurt either way; but at least with it coming from her, she would be able to explain her intentions.

Her cell phone pinged with a message from Ryder.

Are you okay?

Yes. Coming now, she texted back.

Her heart rate had calmed somewhat, but her stomach knots had intensified. She reached into her purse and changed out her hearing aid battery. Then she whispered a prayer for fortitude. Chanel just had to make it through the night. Then she would try to reach Cara and see if she could hurry her sister home.

Ryder swerved into Cara's driveway, glad he had made it back without getting a speeding ticket. But he had a limited amount of time to do what he wanted to get done. He had dropped off Gabby at the children's hour and hadn't stayed because he'd decided to expand Cara's garden as a surprise.

To prepare, Ryder had watched hours of YouTube videos, and he felt confident that he would be able to duplicate what he had seen. The only issue had been when he would get it done.

Then Cara announced she was going to offer an extended story hour every week until Christmas to give parents a chance to shop for presents. Everything was coming together to make this garden come to fruition.

He could work on the garden, knowing that Gabby had proper supervision. Even the weather was cooperating. It was actually sixty-eight degrees on the tenth day of December.

The bags of soil were sitting in the same spotet they'd been in since he gave her lawn the final cut of the season. Cara hadn't started, and this was the best way he knew to thank her since she didn't want financial compensation for training Wolf.

He wanted to do something nice for her, to show how much he valued their friendship.

Because of Cara, he had gone to the church's Thanksgiving potluck, and both he and Gabby had enjoyed the general goodwill of everyone in Hawk's Landing. It had also been his first time attending service in a physical church since his conversion. The result had been an elevated worship experience. Being in the sanctuary when the preacher spoke the Word and when the entire congregation sang praises, he had felt an even deeper and meaningful connection to God.

A few times, Ryder had watched Cara in praise. She had her eyes closed and her hands lifted high as she'd been in communion with God. It had touched him to see her relaxed and carefree as she sang along with the praise team.

He didn't think Cara had noticed it, but Gabby had

mimicked her actions during the worship hour, which Ryder found endearing. At the end of the service, he and Gabby had received hugs and kisses from the members. He'd felt welcomed, and the mothers had jumped in to help with Gabby as they would for their own children. To his surprise, instead of yearning to return to his solitary way of doing things, Ryder had enjoyed the socialization and looked forward to going back again.

Seeing Gabby's face when she was playing with the children had been the greatest deciding factor. That, and the fact that he had returned home with an empty bowl. His coleslaw had been a success.

He strode into Cara's backyard, grabbed the shovel and began loosening the earth. Halfway around the perimeter, Ryder had to race home to get water. Wolf returned with him, yapping at the earthworms, but he was good company.

Ryder stretched his back and neck. It had been a little while since he had done manual labor and his muscles were reminding him of that. He was going to be sore, but for the best reason—helping a friend.

Resting the shovel against her shed, Ryder grabbed the grass rake to further prepare the ground. Once he was done, he used the back of his hand to wipe his brow. By this time, his shirt was streaked with dirt and sweat.

He placed a foot on the grass rake, surveyed his handiwork and smiled. The final phase would be the fencing. Wolf had found a couple of rabbits to chase, and they scampered across the patch of land.

He shook his head. "Enjoy it now, but in an hour, it's a wrap for you guys."

Ryder sauntered over to his truck to get the fencing and posts he had purchased. The ones Cara had bought would not keep out the rabbits or other animals. The grids he would use were one-by-one-inch wire mesh, and the fence was forty-eight inches high. The wire was heavier, vinyl coated and wire welded. According to the YouTube experts, that kind of fencing would last a long time. Before he returned to Cara's yard, he grabbed his measuring tape.

To start erecting the fence, Ryder placed a post into the ground while whistling off-key. This post came with hooks to connect the fence. He bent it so that the animals couldn't dig under and get to the vegetables.

By the time he had finished the fence, Cara was pulling into her driveway. His mouth dropped open, and his first thought was *What time is it?* He wiped his forehead with the back of his hand and dug into his back pocket for his cell phone. Ryder had set a reminder alarm to fetch Gabby when it was time.

He lost his breath. He must have left the phone in the cupholder of his truck. Flipping his wrist, he saw his Apple Watch was dead. Breaking into a sprint, all Ryder could think was that Gabby was at the library, probably scared and waiting for him. In his mind, he saw her alone, crying and screaming his name, though he knew there was no way Cara would leave her alone.

Ryder rushed to the front of the house, Wolf on his heels. "I lost track of time," he huffed out. His heart pounded in his chest, and he couldn't contain his shock that almost three hours had passed so quickly.

Cara gave him a smile full of understanding. "It's quite all right. I tried calling you several times, and when I didn't get you, I decided to bring her home with me. I hope that was okay. After the last time I brought her home, I bought a booster seat so don't worry, she was safe."

She opened the rear door, and Gabby got out. Relief

seeped through him. Of course Cara wouldn't have left Gabby by herself. No one in town would.

"Thank you so much," he said, his shoulders sagging. He wiped the dirt from his hands onto his pants. "And, yes, it is more than okay." Anything was better than his daughter left stranded, in the dark, in an empty parking lot. That was the visual flashing in his brain.

"Hi, Daddy," Gabby said, hugging his leg, her little hands wrapping around him. Unlike Ryder, who was frazzled, she was calm and smiling.

Bending down, Ryder scooped her up in his arms and kissed her cheek. "You okay, pumpkin?"

"Yes. Ms. Cara gave me a ride home because you weren't there yet."

He decided not to alert Gabby to his forgetfulness. Instead, he said, "Yes, and did you say thank you?"

"Thank you, Ms. Cara," she said. Wolf dashed off into the yard, running after a squirrel. "Can I go play with Wolf?"

"Yes, sweetie. But only for a little while. We have to get you in bed for school tomorrow."

Cara approached him, her eyes curious. "What happened?"

Nothing in her tone sounded judgmental, and she hadn't asked what he was doing in her driveway. He took that as an indication of how far their relationship had progressed. Ryder took her hand and asked her to close her eyes.

Then he led her into the backyard. "Open them," he said.

Her eyes widened and she did a jig. "Oh, you put up my fence. Thank you so much. Wow." She marched forward to inspect his work and then walked the circumference, her hand grazing the fence. "This looks amazing. How did you get all this done in three hours?"

"Sheer will," Ryder said with a laugh. He was so glad Cara hadn't snapped at him.

"What made you do this?" she asked, covering her mouth.

"I couldn't think of another way to show you how much I appreciate having you in my life," Ryder said, drawing close. "I didn't know how lonely—how solitary—I was until God gave me Gabby, Wolf and now you. The three of you make my circle complete."

Her eyes glistened. "Did anybody ever tell you, you have a way with words?"

"No, I've been told the opposite, actually," he said, shaking his head.

She chuckled. "Well, they've never heard the way you talk to me."

"No, they haven't. Because I don't speak like this to anyone. At least, not usually," he stammered. "Because you're someone, and I'm talking to you, so…" He trailed off, feeling self-conscious because he doubted she understood what he was trying to communicate. "I'm gonna stop now because I'm not making any sense."

"I understood you perfectly," she said with a soft smile. "I understood every word. Spoken and unspoken." Cara touched his cheek and whispered four words that made his heart warm. "Let's plant seeds together."

Chapter Fifteen

"Who knew that working in the earth could be so therapeutic?" Chanel mused, adjusting the large straw hat on her head.

She was in the garden with Ryder the very next morning, dressed in enough layers to withstand the early-morning chill, though the sun's rays kept her warm.

Ryder had headed over after putting Gabby on the bus, and they'd just finished laying the soil and were ready to plant cabbage, kale, garlic, peas and, of course, more carrots. Those vegetables were hearty enough to withstand winter weather, and the fencing was high enough to keep rabbits from jumping into the garden. She felt confident they would finally reap a good crop this time.

"I agree," Ryder said, running soil through his hands. "I see a powerful message in what we're about to do."

"How so?" she asked, raising a brow and stooping next to him.

"Tilling the earth is akin to giving yourself a new beginning—a rebirth, if you will. And the soil is rich with compost and all different kinds of minerals—a blend of the refuse in our lives that God uses as a foundation to bring new growth."

Chanel nodded, patting the soil with her hands. She had tossed her gloves aside, loving the feel of the smooth earth in her hands. "I can see that." She cocked her head. "Don't tell me you missed your calling—you're preaching this morning."

Quirking his lips, Ryder gave her a light jab. "Quit teasing. You're embarrassing me."

"I'm serious." She straightened. "I used to find working in the garden therapeutic. There's something soothing about this. Getting back to basics."

"There's nothing basic about this."

She cracked up. "Ryder, you need to get out more."

He placed a hand on his chin. "You know, I would be offended if what you said wasn't true. Before you and Gabby, I was a loner, content to remain in my own world. But then Gabby entered my life like a ray of sunshine, ripping apart my orderly existence, and I can't say I regret it one bit." He pointed her way. "And you. You're the pleasant surprise—the cherry on top of the sundae—that I didn't see coming."

Whew. This man. Chanel dabbed the corner of her eyes with the back of her hand. "Okay, you need to quit it with the heartfelt speeches. It's too early for that, and I'm not trying to get dirt in my eyes because you decide to be profound."

"I can't help it. It's your fault for being the best friend on the planet."

Chanel touched her chest, ignoring the twinge that he only saw her as a friend, and held up her other hand. "Any more compliments and I'm going to be a mess." Her heart swelled knowing Ryder held her in such regard. Of course, her fear of his reaction when he learned the truth about her identity ballooned, but she stamped it down. She just had to make sure to be the first to tell him once her sister was safe.

Ryder chuckled and went to retrieve the seedlings in labeled Ziploc baggies. Holding them out, he asked, "Are you ready?"

"Yes. I can't wait to hear what you've got to say about the seeds."

"Jesus already took care of that," he said, referring to the parable of the Sower and the Seed. "I can't mess with perfection." He got on his knees beside her.

She giggled and chose the bag labeled "Carrots." "If I know you, you won't be able to help yourself."

"This from the woman who batted her lashes at me and said, 'Let's plant seeds together,' all breathy, like you were inviting me on the most romantic date in the world."

Date? She'd mull that over later.

Chanel cracked up at Ryder, who had blinked his eyes and mimicked her voice with a much higher, nasally octave.

"I didn't say it *all breathy*." She tossed dirt at him. "And you just proved my point about your needing to get out more if you think this is a date," she added, enjoying their playful banter as friends. "Because wading around in the dirt is definitely not my idea of a date— although, it's been fifteen years, so the dating guidelines might have changed."

Ryder grew serious and turned to face her. "You haven't been on a date in fifteen years?"

"No," she said, swirling her finger in the soil. "It probably sounds pitiful, my mourning a man for that long."

"Is it mourning or guilt?" he asked.

His words hit the center of her heart. "It didn't feel right moving on when I'm the reason Warren died." She splayed out her hands. "We had plans. We were going to work this farm, and then one fateful day changed all that. I think that's why I avoided getting this garden together. A part of me felt like Warren and I should be doing this together."

He grew quiet after that. Contemplative.

Chanel opened one of the seed baggies, sorry she had ruined their lighthearted conversation by talking about Warren. She stuck her finger about an inch deep into the soil and dug a small trench. Ryder squatted beside her to plant his seeds. Side by side, they went down the rows, helping each other as needed, sprinkling the seeds, leaving space between so that the vegetables could grow unimpeded. Then they covered the seeds, patting the earth with their hands. When they were finished, they each placed a marker in the earth.

Chanel watered the seeds. Stepping back, she admired their progress.

Now, she didn't know if it was because Ryder had mentioned the word *date* or because she had not been part of the dating scene for over a decade, but working like this with him felt...intimate. Companionable. *Right.* Guilt over enjoying herself with someone other than Warren filled her.

Ryder released a plume of air, uttered a low, "Hallelujah," wiped his face and stared at her. His gaze held a light heat, and Chanel had to look away. He tucked a hand under her chin to get her to face him. "You were right," he said in a low voice. "I am going to try to add to perfection."

For some reason, her heart raced, and it took a second for her mind to register that he was referring to her earlier comment about the seeds. But she did her best to appear unaffected, which meant she would have to look at him. Dusting off her hands, Chanel tipped her hat so she could see Ryder's eyes.

"Let's have it," she said, her tone playful.

He reached out to touch her curls. "Just now, when we were laying the seeds in the ground, we moved in sync, as a unit. You helped me, and I helped you. I started to see how God brought us together for a greater purpose."

"To restore a vegetable garden?" she asked, her brows furrowed.

"No, silly." He chuckled. "Stay with me." He scooted close. "I don't know your full story, but you know about my parents' abandonment. You had carrot seeds and I had peas." He touched his chin.

Chanel cracked up and gestured her hands between them. "We're like peas and carrots. Different, but we work well together. Is that what you're saying?"

His lips quirked. "I can see I'm rubbing off on you, but there's more."

"Okay, I want to hear it, but this sun is toasting my arms. Why don't we finish up inside?" She got to her feet and held out a hand.

With a nod, Ryder placed his hand in hers and jumped to his feet. They put the garden tools away, and then Chanel escorted him through the back door and into the kitchen. When she entered the house, she thought of Cara and was glad she had listened to her sister and put away the pictures of them together.

Ryder stepped over the threshold and paused.

"What is it?" Chanel asked, washing her hands and then retrieving two glasses for some lemonade. She opened the refrigerator, welcoming the cool blast of air. She was going to take a cold shower later.

"This is my first time coming in here." He sounded humbled. "Thanks for letting me into your home."

"Yeah, well, don't go reading something symbolic into this moment."

His eyes narrowed, though they held mischief. "Stop reading my mind."

He had never imagined a few months ago that he would be inside Cara's home. But here he was—and yes, for him, this was momentous. A home was a sanctuary, a safe place. Only those you trusted should be let inside.

And he found her place charming. Although he would not have thought Cara would be into the frilly kitchen curtains or the rustic white-wood kitchen layout with a barn door, which probably led to a bathroom or pantry. "You have a nice home," he said, eyeing the large plaque over the kitchen table that said Gather Together.

Cara waved a hand and tapped the chair next to her. "I'll give you a tour later. Now, get over here so you can finish telling me what you had to say about the seeds."

He shuffled over to the chair, took a sip of the lemonade and then licked his lips. "I don't know if it's because I'm thirsty, but this is tasting extra delicious."

"Cooking might not be my forte, but I make a wicked-good pitcher of lemonade. Nothing beats freshly squeezed lemons."

Ryder kept drinking until it was gone, then gave a satisfied sigh. "Now, back to what I was saying."

She leaned forward, taking off her hat and placing it on the table.

He began, "As we were planting, God was speaking to my heart. You have your carrots, and I have my peas—which in this analogy represent our past pain. What we did today was bury the seeds of our past pains that we carry every day, that hinder our progress. In this case, Jesus is both the soil and water."

Ryder ran his hands through his hair. "We have to bury our past in Him. He enfolds our pain and showers us with His love. It is only because of His love that we experience new growth. So what this all means is that in order to move forward, we have to bury all the pain of the past. It's the only way we will eventually see the fruit of our labor."

"Wow. That's deep." Cara's eyes appeared misty. "But how do you do that?"

"Sometimes, it means taking a step, like you did today." His heart pounded. For as he spoke to encourage her, he was also talking to himself.

"It means confronting the fear that scares you the most, like perhaps building a garden with someone new." He patted her arm. "I know that garden was something you wanted to do with your husband—on an even grander scale." He touched his chest. "I'm blessed to be the friend that you shared that dream with and made a new memory with. It doesn't replace the old. It's starting the new."

"What's your 'seed'?" she asked, using her fingers as air quotes.

His chest tightened. "My parents' abandonment. I sat in that theater for hours. I told the attendants my parents were coming back. I refused to leave. Because of that, I didn't trust anyone, didn't allow anyone to get close. If no one got close, I couldn't love them and they couldn't hurt me. I wrapped myself in this cocoon of loneliness, not wanting anyone, not needing anyone. But I didn't know I wasn't living. Being afraid isn't living."

He expected compassion, but instead, Cara pursed her lips and kicked back in the chair. "Naw. That's not it."

"What do you mean, that's not it?" His mouth popped open. "That was the most traumatic experience of my life."

"I'm not denying it was traumatic. Horrible, even. It changed the course of your life. How you do things. But your seed today is Christmas."

He lost his breath and shook his head. "We've been through this before. I don't do Christmas."

"Why? What did Christmas do to you?"

Jabbing his index finger on the table, he snarled, "Christmas, the celebrated day of goodwill, was the worst day of my life. That very morning, I sat at the breakfast table. My mother had made a huge breakfast— a farewell feast," he said with bitterness. "She made all my favorites—waffles, scrambled eggs, turkey bacon... She bought chocolate-covered doughnuts."

His breath caught. "My father brought boxes down from the attic. There was a ton of gifts under the tree. I got a bike, Rollerblades, action figures, clothes... Everything you can think of, they bought for me. I opened all these presents, and I was so happy. All I was thinking about was that I couldn't wait to get to school after winter break so I could tell my friends..." Tears slipped past his lids. Choked up, he lowered his chin to his chest, barely able get the words out. "After we opened the gifts, that's when we went to the movies. That's when they left me. For good."

He heard her sniffle. When he glanced her way, he could see that her face was doused with tears.

"I don't get it. Why would they leave?"

"I've asked myself that for years," he croaked. "But I don't have a clear answer. I did some digging, and I think they were in debt and about to lose the house, but that's no excuse."

"That's horrible. Simply horrible." She shook her head. "Why did they go through all the effort of buying all those gifts if they knew they were going to leave?"

His lips curled. "I've thought a lot about that. I think they were buying me gifts for each year of my birthday they would miss." His voice hitched. "As if a bunch of things could make up for losing them. You know what happened to all those presents?"

She cocked her head. "What?"

He lifted his shoulders. "I didn't want them. The social worker brought me home to gather my stuff, and right away, I saw the entire house had been emptied. The only thing left were my clothes, the tree and—" his lips curled again "—the gifts. They had fattened me up, so to speak, knowing they would leave me. This wasn't a random act. It was planned. I bounded up the stairs to get my clothes—the social worker insisted on that. But she couldn't get me to touch those presents… the huge reminders of what I'd lost." His voice broke. "I would have traded them all to get my parents back, to get their love. Every time I see a tree, an ornament, the Christmas wrapping paper, that's all I think about…"

Snatching a few of the napkins off the table, he wiped his face. His heart hurt. He had never shared that with anyone before today. Not even God.

Cara's mouth popped open, forming an O. "Now I understand," she said, nodding. "I get it. I get it. Whew." Fanning her eyes with her hands, she excused herself and ran into the little half bath near the kitchen, shutting the door behind her. Seconds later, he heard her low sobs.

And he knew in that moment, she wasn't crying for herself. She was crying for him—and the little lost boy within.

His heart moved. Closing his eyes, he prayed a single line: "Lord, I give this seed over to You."

When she finally came out of the bathroom, her eyes were puffy and her tone nasal. She stood with her arms about her and whispered, "Thank you for what you did for me today. And for sharing your seed." She cleared her throat. "Come with me. I want to show you something."

He looked at the clock in the kitchen. Was it really only 10:30 a.m.? It felt like he had been baring his soul for hours instead of mere minutes.

Curious, Ryder stood and allowed her to lead him. They walked through the kitchen and into the living room area. He took in her Southern Belle sofa with plush cushions and spindly legs. On the mantel were numerous pictures of Cara with her parents that he would have loved to study, but she was moving.

After opening a door and turning the light on, she took him downstairs to the basement. There was a huge sectional, a coffee table, a full bath and a small room for storage. Bins of all sizes and shapes, neatly labeled. His eyes fell on an oversize gray bin with the name *Warren* written on it in permanent marker.

Cara went to lift it. Ryder raced to assist, toting the bin and following after her. He placed it in the middle of the room as she requested, then squatted to join her on the floor.

Her face had paled and her hands shook, but she opened the bin. Inside were pictures of a tall dark-skinned man with wide shoulders. She pulled out a picture of the two of them and held it up for him to see before resting it next to her. Rummaging around, Cara pulled out a small album.

She opened to the first page, drew in a deep breath and covered her mouth. A two-by-four-inch black-and-white sonogram picture had been preserved underneath the plastic of the photo album, its edges a little yellowed.

"This is my daughter," she whispered, the heartache ringing through her tone. "The one I lost before I got to see her face."

Chapter Sixteen

Ryder didn't know it, but Chanel hadn't been in this basement for over fifteen years. During the past weeks she had been home, she had lacked the courage to venture downstairs. Until today. So this was another milestone. Monumental.

She took the sonogram from under the protective film, and, spotting her name, covered it with her thumb before turning the picture toward him.

"Thanks for sharing it with me. I've never seen one of these up close. I missed this with Gabby," he said, his voice filled with quiet awe.

Chanel smiled, bringing the image close to her chest and taking a deep breath. "She had a strong heartbeat. You should have seen her. Warren and I swore she was showing off. Kelly. That's what we'd decided to call her. We predicted she would be a gymnast, but…she never made it past the womb."

She closed her eyes as the tears fell and swallowed back a sob, knowing this would happen. It felt like her heart was bleeding, and after the way she had cried earlier, Chanel didn't understand how she would have any tears left. She drew deep breaths—inhaling, exhaling, inhaling, exhaling.

Touching her shoulder, he said, "Cara, if this is too hard for you…"

"No. I want to tell you. One good share deserves another," she said, making a feeble attempt at humor. She held up her index finger. "Just give me a minute. I've got to let this all out, or I'm going to burst."

Ryder left for a few seconds before returning and placing tissues in her hand. Squaring her shoulders, she opened her eyes and forced the words out of her mouth.

"It was a beautiful spring day. Warren and I had graduated with our bachelor's degrees in agriculture, and I wanted to celebrate. We went to dinner and stayed up until late, catching up on all the television shows that we had missed while in school on our DVR. We should have slept in the next day, but I insisted we go fishing. Warren was exhausted, but he—he couldn't deny me anything."

Her breath hitched. "If only he hadn't listened. If only I hadn't been so persuasive. If only… If only…" She bit her lower lip and shook her head. "I have gone through that morning several times, trying to decide what I could have done differently."

"You can't," Ryder said. "You can't be the hamster on the wheel, going over and over the *woulda-coulda-shouldas*. At some point, you have to stop seeking, stop searching for answers you will never have."

"Tell that to my conscience." She rubbed her eyes. "So, we took the boat out. The water was calm and the fish were jumping. It was perfect. Until it wasn't." Sighing, she lolled her head back. "Out of nowhere, the weather changed, and the calm day turned into my worst nightmare. Sixty-degree winds whipping our faces, water pelting our skin. Warren was an experienced boater, but he was no match against this thunderstorm.

"Warren tried to lower the sail, to get us back to shore, but the boat rocked so hard that… I fell over." She gazed ahead, focused on the wall before her. "I still remember the freezing water like it was yesterday. And I—I wasn't wearing a life jacket, so he…he reached for me, but the…the sail hit him on the head, and he fell into the water. I struggled to save him… He was going under…" Her chest tightened. "But he was so heavy. I yelled out to God to help me."

Her body shook. Caught up in the memories, Chanel forgot Ryder was there, listening. So when he reached for her hand, she jumped.

"Are you okay?" he said, his eyes filled with worry.

Giving him a jerky nod, she continued, holding his hand like it was a lifeline keeping her in the present so she could talk about her past. Her shivers reduced to a slight tremor.

She licked her chapped lips. "I don't know if it was the shock of the frigid water, but Warren jerked awake, jumped into the boat and pulled me inside. Then he began to take us to shore. I was determined to help, so I stood to give him a hand, and that was when the sail… the sail broke and spliced into my abdomen."

Ryder gasped. "Oh, no. How… Wh—"

"Once he saw I was hurt, Warren shouted over the fury of the winds for me to stay low, remain calm." She snorted. "I had no choice but to listen then. I clutched my stomach, begging Kelly to hold on, pleading with God while Warren got us to shore. Once he pulled that boat to land, he told me that he loved me, dropped to his knees and fell to the earth." Her voice dropped to a whisper. "He never recovered. Dry drowning."

Chanel was surprised that Ryder's eyes were glossy.

"Wow. What a love," Ryder said, overcome. "Oh, Cara, I'm so sorry."

"I must have passed out, because the next time I opened my eyes, I saw bright lights. I had been admitted to the hospital." She faced her neighbor. "He died trying to save me. And he *did* save me. But I lost them both, two of the most precious people to me—my husband and my child—and all I have been left with is this over-whelming guilt and the nightmare of reliving that day over every night. My own personal *Groundhog Day*."

Ryder yawned and stretched his neck. He had been in his office since 3:30 a.m. working on a rough draft of an article documenting the results of his team's recent research. He was the lead author and wanted to submit the paper as soon as possible to the Journal of Cancer Research and Clinical Oncology. His hope was to get the draft done before the New Year.

When he wasn't working, Ryder's mind was occupied with Gabby's hearing loss and Cara. Cara's heart-wrenching story of her loss had stayed with him. When he had left her home a week ago, he was drained. Emotionally and physically.

It hadn't been easy for either of them, taking that first step, opening the lid on the past, freeing all the hurt…remembering. But it was necessary for healing. Since that day, they had prayed together every morning over the phone. Like peas and carrots. Every day, the boulder on his chest eased, and he hoped that was the case with his friend.

Glancing at his cell phone, he could see it was 5:55 a.m.

Ryder rushed to brush his teeth, knowing Cara would be calling in exactly five minutes for their morning prayer. While he brushed, he read the three words he had scrawled on a Post-it and placed on his bathroom mirror. *Companionship. Comfort.* That's what he sought. One he found in Cara and the other in God.

Closure. That's what he needed.

Today, his heart pounded thinking about a special favor he wanted to ask of Cara and hoped he wouldn't lose courage.

For him, the task seemed daunting, but he knew Cara would be up for the challenge.

Just as he was rinsing his mouth, the phone rang. He wiped his mouth and rushed to answer. Seeing her name on his screen was like a shot of espresso. He bounded into his bedroom and plopped on the edge of his bed.

"I have a Scripture this morning," she said once he had responded. "Jeremiah 29, verse 13, says, 'And ye shall seek me, and find me, when ye shall search for me with all your heart.'"

Pulling up the Bible app on his phone, Ryder highlighted the verse. "What I like about this verse is that it uses the word *shall*. That means there is no doubt that it will happen."

They took a few minutes to expound on the verse before they each prayed. When they were finished, Ryder cradled his phone to his ear, stood, and squared his shoulders. "Cara, before you go, I wanted to ask for your help with something."

"What do you need?" she asked without hesitation.

He paced the room. "I—I…" Why was this so hard? Ryder thought of the little girl sleeping down the hall from him and knew he needed to push through.

"Take your time," Cara said.

"I need help with Christmas," he rushed out. "I want to give Gabby the holiday she wants, but I don't know what to do. It might be asking a lot, but I'm hoping you would help me with it. I want to make a new memory. I want to see her smiling face."

"I'd be glad to," she squealed. "Oh, Ryder, I'm so glad you changed your mind. I think it's really brave." He could hear her clapping her hands, and despite his trepidation, he smiled. "I'm going to help you give Gabby a Christmas to remember."

He just hoped it would be one he survived.

Chapter Seventeen

"I have my list and I've checked it twice," Cara said, all smiles, wearing a Santa hat, a red turtleneck and jeans. She stood in the aisle of Christmas ornaments, inspecting each of the round balls before placing them in the cart. She scrunched her nose. "It's a good thing we came today, because if we had waited any longer, we would have the reject pile. As it is, these are slim pickings. The best time to shop for Christmas is actually at the *end* of Christmas, when everything is on sale. I am usually able to get one or two good pieces to add to my collection."

Ryder turned his back so she wouldn't see his eye roll. To his inexperienced eye, there was nothing wrong with the ornaments—she was being picky. This had to be the fifth store she had dragged him to, and he was beyond exhausted. The crowd, the music and a Santa collecting donations in every store drained him. And what was up with every single store smelling like peppermint spice?

His neighbor, on the other hand, seemed energized. If this was her version of "running a few errands," he didn't want to know what a full-on shopping spree would feel like. As soon as he had put Gabby on the bus, Cara had been ready to go.

At one point, he had thought about giving Cara his Amex card and telling her to have at it, but then Ryder had pictured Gabby's face. For her sake, he kept going. And going. And going. They had purchased a gingerbread-house kit, popcorn, cranberries and string, stockings, yard decorations, and a bunch of other items that Cara had stressed they would need.

Their plan was to decorate the house when Gabby was in school. He mopped his brow, mentally preparing himself for the electric bill.

At least the weather would be cooperative. The rest of the week would be sunny and close to fifty degrees. Delaware weather was like a seesaw, though—one day it could be in the thirties and the next, close to seventy. Ryder made sure he and Gabby took their vitamin C to boost their immune system.

Both he and Cara had agreed that Gabby should choose the Christmas tree. They would do that the next day.

"I haven't found a star," Cara said.

"Let me check the boxes on the top shelf." He lifted one of the unopened boxes.

"Can we do that?" she asked, looking around with a furtive glance.

He shrugged. "I just did. I'm sure the owners won't care. For them, it's a sale." Using his key, he cut through the clear masking tape.

Raising a brow, she pointed between them and said, "You and I don't have the same privilege."

"I know," Ryder said, acknowledging and understanding her reference to her race. He had noticed the extra glances Cara received when they entered a store outside of town where she wasn't known. And he had seen people relax when they realized she was with him.

Digging through the box of various Christmas items, Ryder held up an angel, puffing out his chest like he had struck gold.

"Wonderful," she exclaimed.

She examined it before giving him her nod of approval. Ryder placed it in the cart. Humming "Jingle Bells" under her breath, Cara wandered down the aisle, picking up this or that and putting it back. Ryder leaned against the shelf and pulled up an article to read until she exhaled. "All right, let's get out of here."

Swinging the cart around, he sped to the front of the store, ignoring Cara's chuckle behind him. She must have sensed he was rushing to check out before she decided to look at more decorations.

His stomach was growling, and it was time to eat. The apple and muffin Cara had given him from her purse had long worn off. It was time to refill.

Once they'd paid and Ryder had packed all their goods inside the truck, Ryder jumped into the vehicle, glad for the warmth.

To his surprise, Cara held out a reindeer hat for him.

He lifted a hand. "Whoa, where are you going with that?"

"I got it for you so you could get into the season," she said, waving the hat back and forth. "It even plays music. See?" She pressed a button that made the lights come on and the reindeer ears dance.

Yeah. Not doing that.

Splaying his hands toward their purchases, he said, "My wallet can testify that I am very much into the season."

"Oh, don't be a Grinch," she teased, waggling her brows.

He cocked his head. "This really is your favorite season, isn't it?"

She nodded. "I love the weather, the singing, the traditions…everything." For a second, her eyes dimmed. "I was working long hours and didn't really do a lot during the holidays for a while. It's not as much fun celebrating alone… Now, are you going to put this on?"

Snatching the hat, he placed it on his head. "Happy now?"

"Yup. It goes perfectly with your brown sweater and jeans." Taking out her phone, she scooted close and snapped a picture of them together. Her hair had a light grapefruit scent, which he found he liked. Cara backed out of the parking lot. "Let's get lunch."

"Okay, but it will have to be a grab-and-go because I have to be home to meet Gabby when she gets off the bus."

"Or maybe you can make us sandwiches while I work on the inside decorations."

Ryder agreed though he couldn't help but think how much he and Cara were acting like a unit. That didn't bother him. In fact, it made him feel…anticipation and a sense of belonging. He couldn't wait to see Gabby's face when she got home.

Okay, so maybe she had gone overboard—or, as she would phrase it, *exceeded expectations*. They had unpacked her truck, and all the decorations and supplies covered Ryder's living room floor. With only an hour until Gabby got off the bus, Chanel knew they would have to be strategic. Christmas was a week away, and they were trying to do what usually took weeks in mere days.

Still yet, Ryder had looked to her, and she was determined not to fail him.

Chanel placed a hand on her hip and gave Ryder a tentative smile. "So, I know this looks like a lot, but if we work together, we can have this done in no time."

He gave her a skeptical look, gesturing at all the Christmas paraphernalia. "I've led many research teams, but this is on another level. Frankly, it feels daunting." Holding up his iPad Mini and Apple Pencil, he scratched his head. "I was going to take notes for next year, but I think I'll need to keep my hands free."

"Let's break this task down into small, manageable pieces," she said in a gentle tone. "Take a deep breath, and tackle the gifts first. You went all out, and wrapping all these gifts is going to take time. I propose we put these in your bedroom closet or somewhere Gabby won't find them. Then we can wrap them when she's asleep."

His lips quirked.

"What?" she asked, raising a brow.

"I'm so glad you're using words like *we*, because I sure couldn't do this on my own."

Her heart warmed. "I'm happy to help, friend." She rubbed her hands together. "Now, let's get a move on."

After toting all the gifts and all the wrapping paper up to Ryder's room, they started wrapping the garland with lights around the banister. Then they decorated the mantel with more garland, elves and stockings with Ryder's, Gabby's and Wolf's names. Ryder had used the iron to steam the letters, and she noticed he had them perfectly centered, with equal spacing between each letter.

Tears sprang to Chanel's eyes when Ryder put up a fourth stocking bearing Cara's name. She appreciated his thoughtful gesture but felt a pang over the fact that it was for the wrong sister. She would have loved to see her name on the wall.

"When did you get that extra stocking?" she asked when they started bagging the trash. "I was right there by the cash register."

He placed a finger over his lips. "I'll never tell."

She chuckled and glanced around the room. The train set was tucked into the corner, waiting to be assembled, and Ryder had cleared the coffee table for the gingerbread house. They would put that together on Christmas Eve. The outdoor decorations had been relocated to the porch, and they would do that this evening or tomorrow—depending on how the tree-shopping went.

She released a breath. "It looks twenty times better in here."

"I'm glad. I wouldn't have been able to sleep tonight with the chaos." He had seemed worried at first. She'd seen his face pale at the mess in the living room and thought he was about to pass out.

"I told you, I got this," she bragged.

Suddenly, he gasped and took off for the front door. Wolf came running from the kitchen and chased after him to meet Gabby at the bus stop. Her eyes went wide. Gabby's bus. Chanel waited for their return, making sure her camera was on to capture Gabby's face when she saw the decorations.

She kept the camera trained on the door. Gabby came in first, and when she saw Chanel, she squealed.

"Hi, Ms. Cara." She raced over to give Chanel a hug. Her body landed against Chanel's with such force that she had to grip her phone tight to keep it from falling.

"Hey, how was school?"

Jumping up and down, the little girl said, "Good. We

learned how to spell words that end with *at*. Like *cat*, *bat*—and guess what? This boy in my class, he said, 'attack.'" Gabby cracked up. "*Attack* isn't an *at* word. It was so funny."

Hearing her giggles made Chanel and Ryder laugh. She kept the video recording but met Ryder's eyes. He lifted his hands, silently communicating that he didn't know why Gabby hadn't spotted the decorations as of yet.

"Let me get your coat," Ryder said, holding a hand out.

Gabby took off her scarf, placed a finger on the zipper of her coat and then gasped. Her eyes brightened and she dashed over to the mantel, seeming to forget about her coat, the scarf trailing behind her.

"Look! Look!" she yelled. "This is Christmas. We're having Christmas. Yay!" Racing over to the stairs, her voice boomed, "This is so nice." She clapped her hands and ran back over to the mantel.

Wolf danced along with her, his tail wagging.

Chanel sure wished she had some of Gabby's energy because she was tired. Good tired. The joy on the little girl's face made their morning dash worth it. Her eyes glistened when she saw Gabby so excited.

"Yes, do you see the stocking with your name on it?" Chanel prompted, beckoning for Ryder to join her by the mantel.

"Ohhhhh," Gabby said, twirling around, a ball of energy. "Guess what, guess what? I can spell it. G-a-b-b-y." Wolf barked along with her like he was also trying to spell, but Gabby ignored him. "My name is Gabrielle, but everyone calls me Gabby."

Ryder laughed. "Yes. I also call you *sweetie* and *honey*."

Giggling, she lifted her head up toward Ryder. "Mommy calls me *baby* too. I have a lot of names."

"Well, you have a lot of *nick*names," Ryder corrected.

Chanel stopped the video and captured a picture of that father-daughter moment. She was going to print out a copy and frame it. Ryder didn't have any pictures of himself and Gabby on display. She swallowed a secret smile. Now she knew what to get him for Christmas, besides the sweater she had planned.

"Wow!" Gabby yelled. "Ms. Cara, here is one for you too." She proceeded to spell Cara's name, Wolf's and her father's.

"Are you hungry?" Ryder asked his daughter. "We made sandwiches."

"No, I had my fruit on the bus," she said in her version of a whisper. "We aren't supposed to eat on the bus, but I was really, really, really hungry."

Shaking her head, Chanel couldn't hold back her chuckle. Ryder couldn't either, although he did admonish her for not following the rules.

"Well, since you're not hungry, how about we go look for a Christmas tree?" Ryder put on his coat and handed Chanel hers.

"Yes," Gabby said, pumping her fists.

"Let me guess—you always wanted to do that," Ryder said in a dry tone, moving to the front door in long strides. He sent Wolf to his place, and the dog let out a pitiful wail. Chanel's heart twisted, but Wolf would only be a distraction, and many people feared dogs of his size.

"How did you know I was going to say that, Daddy?" Gabby yelled, following after him, dragging her scarf on the floor.

"Hmm. Just a guess."

Chanel shook her head at Gabby's wonder. This little girl was so entertaining. So precious.

She honestly didn't understand how her mother had stayed away from her for so long. If Gabby were hers, she would be with her 24-7, soaking up that joy.

That's how it goes, she supposed. Those who had it didn't always want it—or appreciate it. And those who wanted it didn't always get it—or lost it.

Chapter Eighteen

Since it was early afternoon at Fifer Orchards, there weren't too many people milling about, so they should find a decent tree in no time. When they pulled into the lot and climbed down from the truck, Gabby took both Chanel's and Ryder's hands. The owner waved and told them to pick out a tree. Once they decided, one of his team members would cut it down and place it in her pickup.

Chanel shivered. The weather had cooled to about thirty-seven degrees.

Pulling on their hands, Gabby shouted and pointed down an aisle. "I see a really big one. Let's go over there."

Chanel craned her neck. "Whoa."

It was really high. Too high.

"That one's too big, honey," Ryder said, squinting. "We need one that can fit into Ms. Cara's pickup and our house." He gestured to another lane. "Let's look down here and see if you find one that you want."

"I want one that's nice and fluffy."

"Fluffy?" Chanel asked, treasuring the feel of the little hand wrapped around hers.

They passed a family, and it struck her how, to others, they probably appeared to be a family as well. She slid a glance in Ryder's direction. He had those baby blues pinned on her and was giving her a crooked-lip smile—like Elvis Presley. Her heart lost its natural rhythm because of that look.

"Yeah, I don't want it to be hungry," Gabby said.

Maybe she was making too much out of his expression. She broke eye contact and zoned in on Gabby's words. "Hungry?" Then she understood. "Oh, you mean you want a nice, full tree."

"Yeah. Because then, when you put on the balls and stringy stuff, it will make it look nice."

"I completely agree," Ryder said. He stopped in front of an eight-foot tree and asked, "What you think of this one?"

Eyeing it, Chanel thought he had chosen a good one. But Gabby didn't seem impressed.

The little girl scrunched her nose, "Uh, I don't know."

Chanel's and Ryder's eyes connected over her head. This time, she knew for sure she didn't mistake the warmth in his blue orbs. She played with her curls and told herself to act normal. Unbothered.

But she *was* bothered. And not in a bad way. Her insides warmed, nice and slow—like the seat warmers in her pickup. The feeling wasn't overwhelming. Just pleasant.

"Why don't you think about it?" Ryder said. He was talking to Gabby but looking at Chanel.

It was like they were having a nonverbal conversation of their own. Chanel's heart rate accelerated, and she felt a little warm under her coat.

"Maybe you should walk around the entire tree and

do a proper investigation before you make up your mind," Chanel suggested.

Gabby took her advice, but she decided to hop around the tree instead, declaring that she was the Christmas bunny.

"Somebody has their holidays mixed up," Chanel said with a laugh.

Ryder nodded, watching his daughter with delight on his face. "I think she's going to sleep really good tonight."

"Yup, she'll probably fall asleep as soon as we get back on the road. I know it's going to take more than twenty minutes to get home because of the holiday traffic." Now she was rambling.

Stuffing her hands into her coat pockets, Chanel walked to the end of aisle under the pretense of looking at trees to put some space between them. What was going on right now? Ryder was looking at her like... like she was more than a friend.

She wasn't quite sure how she felt about that. Especially since she hadn't told him the truth about who she was. Or in this case, who she wasn't. Her insides fluttered. Chanel didn't know how she was going to begin that conversation.

By the way, Ryder, I have a funny story to tell you... Or, *Ryder, you know how you said there was something different about me? You were right.* She sighed. Any way she looked at it, the very necessary conversation would be awkward. And there was a strong possibility that the truth would end their friendship.

A hand on her back made her jump.

"You okay?" Ryder asked, suddenly standing beside her.

"Yeah, yeah." Slightly flustered, she lifted a hand. "Just looking at trees."

"This scrawny one?"

Her eyes went wide. She was standing by what had to be the saddest, sorriest tree in the lot. Rather than answer him, she looked around for Gabby. Spotting her a couple trees away, Chanel relaxed.

"Did you find a tree?"

"She's still looking," he whispered. He touched her cheek. "I think she's going to end up with the original one I picked out."

"I don't think she will," Chanel said, skittering away. The spot where his finger had touched her sizzled. "I'm going to see if I can persuade her to change her mind."

He chuckled, eyes narrowed, "You don't play fair, Cara Shelton."

"I play to win."

In the end, Gabby chose the scrawny tree, even though it looked hungry, stating that it needed rescuing because no one else would choose it. Chanel had to admit that her heart melted like gold under fire when Gabby uttered those words.

All she could think was, no matter what happened when Ryder learned the truth, she would never regret getting to know this precious little girl.

Ryder tucked Gabby under the covers and touched her cheek. She actually had a smile on her face, and his heart warmed knowing he had helped put it there. After they had purchased the tree, they went with Cara to her story hour—the last one until after the New Year. Then he had prepared dinner.

The barbecue chicken had been seasoned perfectly, and his garlic green beans had been a good addition. Cara had made some of her lemonade, adding raspberry syrup to the mix, and the result had been a delicious meal.

Then all three of them decorated the tree. By the time they were finished, Gabby was tuckered out, so he took her upstairs to bed and Cara left for home.

Ryder walked down the hallway to his bedroom. He could admit he hadn't been ready for Cara to go yet. Maybe it was time he acknowledged that somehow, in the midst of growing their friendship, a different kind of seed had been planted.

Attraction.

When they were in the orchards, he had struggled to keep his eyes off her. He could only hope she didn't notice, because Cara appeared to be still in love with her husband after all these years. That showed her loyalty—which for him, whose parents chose to run instead of raising him, meant something.

His cell phone rang.

It was Brittany calling on FaceTime. He pressed the accept button. "Hey, Gabby just fell asleep. Do you want me to wake her?"

"No, I called to talk to you, anyway." Her eyes looked troubled, her face drawn.

His stomach muscles clenched. "What's going on?"

"I won't make it back for Gabby's surgery," she said, her voice dull.

Ryder plopped on his bed. He had emailed her with an update, and she had responded that she would be there. "Brittany, you're her mother. She's going to need you here."

Chewing on her bottom lip, she averted her eyes and appeared to look guilty. "You know this life. It's just that another amazing opportunity came up, and I've got top consideration to join the expedition."

"And your daughter is having an operation. I don't think there's any question of what you should do." Ryder hated coming at her that way, but all he could think about was Gabby's face when she heard her mother wouldn't be there. He knew firsthand what it was like to have your parents crush your expectations.

Brittany appeared pensive. "What about Cara? Gabby likes her. Do you think she should go?"

"Are you serious?" he sputtered. "I can't believe you would even suggest that." Cara was going to be there, of course, but she wasn't Gabby's mother. She wasn't the one Gabby would want there the most. He couldn't believe he would have to explain that.

"I'm trying to juggle everything," she said, eyes filling with tears. Her lips quivered. "This is my livelihood. I've got to work to support her."

His brows shot up. "Really?"

"Not now, of course," she said, waving a hand. "But if this excavation is successful, I'll be set for life and so will Gabby." He could see the sparkle, the hunger, in her eyes and knew that meant Brittany had made her choice.

"There will always be one more thing," he said. "It's about priorities."

Her face twisted. "Don't tell me about priorities. What right do you have to judge me?"

"I wasn't trying to judge. Just give me full custody or even shared custody," Ryder said. "You can come see Gabby whenever you want. But she needs stability, and I'm willing to give that to her."

"Okay," she said. His chest eased. "We can talk legalities, but I need you to understand that I love my daughter." Then she asked, "Will you tell Gabby that I won't be there for me?"

So she was leaving him with the horrible task of disappointing their daughter. He released a long breath. "Yeah. I'll let her know."

Someone called out her name, and Brittany muted herself to talk to them. When she came back on, she said, "I-I've got to get going, but let Gabby know I love her." Before he could respond, she ended the call.

Once he was off the phone, Ryder showered and got into bed, debating whether or not he should take legal action in case she changed her mind. He didn't want to go for full custody, because Brittany had been a good mother to Gabby before he knew about her. Although, judging from what Gabby said, his daughter had had to fend for herself a lot because of Brittany's preoccupation with her job. He knew how intense on-site expeditions could be—and how exhilarating. It was no place for a five-year-old, which was why Brittany had brought Gabby to him. That was the best decision she could have made. Yet it still benefitted her own interests.

Crossing his legs, he sighed. Though he'd only had Gabby for a few months, the love he felt for her, the desire to protect her and the knowledge that he would do anything for her intensified with each passing day. Rubbing his eyes, he decided to add this issue to his prayer list.

A text came through from Cara. I'd like to invite you and Gabby to a movie night at my house tomorrow.

What's the movie?

It's a Wonderful Life. Seen it?

No.

Ryder didn't own a television. On purpose. They brought back too many memories of that day in the movie theater. He remembered being so involved in the movie that he hadn't even noticed his parents hadn't returned. Since then, he avoided movies and TV shows. He preferred live shows and performances. And he watched YouTube videos on his laptop or cell phone when needed.

It had been years since he watched a movie for entertainment and not information. Another text came through.

Gabby will enjoy it and you can't have a great Christmas without a great Christmas movie.

Tapping the phone on his thigh, Ryder considered Cara's request. Only because it was her. Anyone else, he would have already declined out of habit. But it *was* her. And that made all the difference in his mind.

Yes, we'd love to come.

He sent his response before he could change his mind. Then he smiled. He was looking forward to spending more time in her company. She made him feel uplifted, and Gabby thrived in her presence. Thinking about that made Ryder remember Brittany's suggestion that he ask Cara to accompany him and Gabby to the surgery.

You bring the popcorn.

He chuckled. Afraid you'll burn it? Cara had told him she wasn't a good cook. He guessed that also transferred over to snacks.

Whatever, she texted back.

Cracking up, he swiped, You didn't even try to deny it.

He watched the three dots appear and eagerly awaited her response.

Are you trying to have the last word? she asked.

LOL. Yeah.

Just give it up. See you tomorrow.

Okay, he fired back, laughing when she sent a shrugging Memoji. He shrugged back.

Stop texting!

Holding his stomach as he laughed, he texted, Okay.

Cara must have conceded, because she hit the "Like" button. Right before he closed his eyes, he sent her his own Memoji, throwing a kiss.

Chapter Nineteen

Decisions, decisions.

Chanel loved huge screens. The larger the screen, the better. Which was why, when it came to her impulse purchase, she had no regrets. She had spent most of the morning giving the house a good clean before going out to do her Christmas shopping. She had purchased an absurd number of clothes for Gabby and a camera for Cara. Then she had hunted for the perfect gadget to place in Ryder's stocking since she had already framed and wrapped his picture.

That's when she encountered the must-have television at a great price.

Looking around the living room, which already boasted a fifty-five-inch, she wondered where she would put the seventy-five-inch Samsung QLED television she had just purchased. Maybe she should set it up in the basement and repurpose the space as a family entertainment room. She tapped her feet. Or should she move the fifty-five-inch to the basement and set this up here?

Something else she couldn't decide on was Ryder's last text.

All throughout the day, Chanel had obsessed over his kiss Memoji. What did he mean by it? Was he just goading her by having the last word, or did he mean to send her a real kiss? There was no way she was going to ask, though. Ryder might think she saw something he'd meant in jest as significant.

Ugh. It was perplexing—and sort of exciting. She felt like a schoolgirl instead of a woman of forty-one. The last time she had experienced this kind of excitement was when she and Warren were dating. Except there was no texting back then. But there was the note reading, "Do you want to go out with me? Circle yes or no." She cracked up. Boy, had she been glad she'd circled yes.

If only he were here to share these moments and reminisce...

But he wasn't. And Ryder was...

She waited for the pang. The usual guilt. But none came. Instead, she felt...hope.

Why?

Her heart rate increased, and her palms became sweaty. Chanel shoved that question out of her mind. Better to go back to the TV decision. That's one that was solvable in this moment...and safer.

She decided to call Ryder and see if he was available. Their morning prayers had expanded to mini-conversations, and she found she liked his decisiveness. He said he'd be there in twenty minutes after he dropped Gabby off at winter camp at the church.

Chanel dashed up the stairs to brush her teeth and hair and slide some lip gloss over her lips. Looking into her bathroom mirror, she laughed. All this because of a kiss Memoji? She snapped her fingers and dashed into her bedroom to spritz herself with perfume.

Her cell phone rang, and she dug it out of her jeans pocket. She frowned. It was her old job calling.

"Hi, Chanel," her former boss said. "I'm calling because I wanted to let you know there's a new position opening up. Mine. I just found out I'm going to be a grandmother, so I'm going to retire to help with the baby. I wanted to ask if you'd be interested in taking over the library. Things with Alma didn't work out… Since you interviewed less than three months ago, I'm recommending to the board that we forego the interview, as you're my top candidate. I know I can leave the library in your hands."

Look at God. She had been rejected but now she had a chance at being restored. Chanel didn't even ask what happened with Alma. She was grateful for the consideration.

Chanel walked down the stairs in a daze. "First, congratulations, Suzanne. I'm happy for you. Second, I'm honored you thought of me." She fiddled with her hair and looked around. Thinking about Ryder and Gabby and her garden, she found herself hesitating. "May I have some time to think about it?" she asked.

"Absolutely. How about you give me your answer after Christmas?" Suzanne suggested.

Chanel agreed. Once the call ended, she broke out into an excited jig, doing some old moves, like the Wop and the Snake.

Then her doorbell rang. Ryder. Her chest heaved from her exertion. Her hair! She couldn't begin to wonder what it must look like. She ran her fingers through her curls and dashed to answer the door. When she saw his smiling face, she was still so excited about the job offer, she gave him a spontaneous hug.

For those few seconds, she allowed herself the luxury of being in his arms. Her insides fluttered. When his arms wrapped around her, she soaked it in, inhaling his woodsy scent. This was her first voluntary contact with a man other than Warren, and it was all the feels and none of the regrets.

Ryder patted her back. "As much as I like our new way of greeting, I've got to get back to work. What's going on?"

She jumped out of his arms, knowing her cheeks were brick red. Covering her embarrassment, she turned away from him and marched into the living room. "I need you to help me make up my mind. Do you think this television would work in here, or should I set it up in the basement?"

"Definitely the basement." He walked over to the oversize box, then faced her, his eyes wide. "Please don't tell me you carried this in here by yourself."

"Okay, I won't," she quipped.

He lifted the box. "Okay, it's not too heavy."

"Yes, they're making televisions lighter than air nowadays."

"I wouldn't know, as I don't own one," he huffed, half lifting, half dragging the box to the basement.

"I noticed that," she said, taking up the rear while they maneuvered the monster-sized box into the basement.

Since she had purchased a wall mount and had the right tools, Ryder set up her television on the wall. Stepping back, he chuckled. "I guess this is what they mean by 'go big or go home.'"

They shared a laugh, but Chanel mulled over his words while she got things ready for their movie night. Maybe it was time she did the same. Make a big move with Ryder—like returning his kiss Memoji in person and telling him who she really was. Telling him the truth about her identity would be the perfect gift.

"I loved it," Ryder said to Cara once the movie ended. She lay snuggled against him on the right, her head on his shoulder, while Gabby was asleep to his left, her head on his lap. When he and Gabby had arrived, they'd played card games before settling into the movie with popcorn and Cara's delicious lemonade.

She had set up surround sound speakers, so it was a theater-like experience. He'd expected to feel some anxiety but he hadn't, which Ryder attributed to his current company.

"I'm so glad because this is a classic and an example of epic storytelling," she said, placing a hand on her chest and turning to face him. He watched her dab at her eyes. "It gets to me every time. The fact that George Bailey had a full life and had impacted so many others and didn't know it."

Nodding at her insight, Ryder said, "That's so true. Sometimes, we're so busy running after what we think we want—fame, fortune or the next big thing—and we don't realize we have to stop and appreciate our life now, for what…" he lowered his voice "…or who is right in front of us."

They made eye contact as tension rose between them. She hadn't returned his kiss Memoji. Wasn't she as curious as he was to learn if they had a more intimate connection? Their friendship meter was already off the chart.

She fidgeted. "Every time I watch this film, I wonder what would happen if life gave me a second chance. Would I choose differently?" Cocking her head, she asked, "Would you want a do-over?"

Raising a brow, he said, "That's a good question." He scrunched his nose and pondered it. "It's hard to say. I thought my obvious answer would be yes, but then my path wouldn't have led me to my daughter…or you."

"Oh," she breathed out. He could see her cheeks flush from his direct response.

He rushed to put her at ease. "I mean, I value our friendship, and my life has only gotten better since you've come into it. You're a pleasant surprise."

She bit her lower lip and nodded, keeping her gaze from his so he couldn't tell what she was feeling. Maybe his directness made her shy.

Cara, shy?

He couldn't imagine that. She was probably just thinking about what he'd said.

"What a wonderful compliment." She finally made eye contact. "I'm glad I got to know you as well. You're more than I thought you would be…"

The air tightened.

He moved closer, touched her chin and whispered, "What about you? What would you want to change?"

She had closed her eyes when he asked the question. They popped open, and she gave an awkward laugh. He held back a chuckle, knowing she had expected him to kiss her. If his daughter wasn't snoring and drooling on him, he sure would have.

Slapping her leg, she recovered and said, "That's easy. I would wish for my husband and daughter to be alive. I wonder what Kelly would be like. She would be fifteen. How we would get along…?" She trailed off, staring at the screensaver on the television screen.

"So many things…" Then she shrugged. "But this is life. How do I know my marriage would have lasted? Would either be alive today, or would another tragedy have occurred?" She shook her head. "The more I think about the what ifs, the more I am realizing I don't know anything." She paused for a few beats before releasing a breath. "Wow."

Her eyes widened like she had just come to a realization.

"What? What's going on in that pretty brain of yours?" He dared to touch her head; then he had to touch her hair, her cheek.

"I've been tormenting myself with that question for years. It has caused me so much guilt. But I'm seeing there's no way of knowing, even if they had survived, that we would be one big happy family today. I can't re-write history…" Her eyes had a sheen to them. "I guess I just have to accept what is." Now she rested a hand on Ryder's face, cupping her palm against his cheek. "I finally see what the message was about."

Heat flooded his face. She was looking at him with warmth in her eyes and with expectation, but his brain was foggy. Ryder struggled to keep up with their conversation, to remember what she had said. "I'm going to need you to repeat that last part, but I need a minute."

Her lips quirked.

Ryder gave himself a mental shake. He needed to put space between them. If he didn't, he wouldn't be able to carry on a coherent conversation, and he had a feeling what she was about to say was important. He lifted Gabby off his leg and placed her on the couch, then stood.

Gabby stretched before curling her body into a comfortable position. Cara scooted over so his daughter had enough room.

Placing his hands on his hips, he asked, "Now, can you repeat what you said?"

She stood as well. Coming to touch his arm, Cara

said, "I said I understand what the message was about in the YouTube video you had me watch."

He nodded. "Oh, okay."

"I understand that acceptance is a part of being healed from the past. The more you question, the more you stay in limbo. Never moving forward and never able to go backward either. To truly live in the present, and even for the future, we have to accept the past for what it is—the past. And we can't give it power over the future."

He ran his hands down his face and nodded. "Having you in my life does make it easier to do."

"Thank you. I feel the same for you," she said, her smile wide. "Our friendship has been a blessing in so many ways. This is what the Bible meant when it said, 'Two are better than one; because they have a good reward for their labor.'" She splayed her hands. "This is my roundabout way of saying, my life is better with you in it."

His heart thumped in his chest. He could see the sincerity in her eyes. "We're peas and carrots…an unlikely combination that works."

Cocking her head, Cara said, "But there's an underlying tension between us that I feel tonight." She stepped closer, touching his sweater. Her brows furrowed. "What do you suppose that it is?"

He laughed, positive she knew the answer to that question. He tucked his finger under her chin. "You never did return my kiss Memoji."

Licking her lips, she said, "I figured I would return it in person."

"Bold move…" he challenged.

Now his heart sped faster than the rabbit jumping her old fence. He wanted to snatch her in his arms, but Ryder sensed he had to let Cara move at her own pace. She took a tentative step closer, and he prayed she wouldn't notice how fast his chest was rising and falling. Her arms circled him, and she rested her head against his.

Squeezing him, she said, "It's been years since I've held a man like this."

He wrapped his arms around her, cradling her head and rocking her. They danced to an imaginary tune. Then she went on her tiptoes and pressed a light, tentative kiss on his lips.

Ryder tightened the embrace, holding her tenderly, allowing her to explore. He felt a light trickle—her tears—on his lips, and he knew in that moment, she was saying goodbye to Warren and hello to possibilities.

To him.

Cupping her head, he took over, deepening the kiss, wanting her to think of him now.

Only of him.

And this wonderful kiss.

Chapter Twenty

While Gabby was at camp, Ryder decided to go on a hunt. He needed to find the ultimate gift for Cara. One that summated how he felt about their friendship and her. Though he had ordered a HomePod Mini from Apple for her stocking, her actual gift was too important to order online. He needed to see and touch whatever he chose to make sure it felt right. As right as he'd felt when his lips had been pressed to hers.

Which is why he had driven up to the Christiana mall as soon as he had finished his article and submitted it to the team for revision.

The parking lot was so full, he had to park at the movie theater and trek across the lot to the mall. He wasn't complaining, though. He had been fortunate to snag that spot.

The weather was brisk, windy and had a distinct chill that made him wonder if it might snow. Hunching down into his coat, he pulled his cap lower on his head, meandering past the cars until he arrived at the entrance.

Opening the door, his ears were filled with the loud buzz of conversations and Christmas music. He stopped, taking in the huge number of people in the mall. *'Tis the season*, he thought. To his left was the food court, and a Barnes & Noble bookstore was to the right.

Sauntering into the bookstore, he bought Cara a gift card since he knew she liked to read. Another stocking stuffer. He patted his coat pocket. Now to find the present that was a physical representation of how he felt.

Hold on a second. How *did* he feel? Ryder stopped mid-step. He knew he was attracted to Cara's mind, her beauty—but did he have deeper feelings than that? The throng pressed around him, but he hardly noticed. When it came to Cara, he experienced a whirlwind of emotions—all good. Forcing his legs to move, he wondered, could this be love?

That question gnawed at him while he searched. Ryder didn't know what he was looking for, but he would know once he had found it. For the next hour, he checked out perfumes, dress shoes, sweaters, watches… But nothing expressed the depth of his emotion. Panic lined his stomach. He swallowed. He had to find something within the next twenty minutes because he needed enough travel time to pick up Gabby from winter camp.

He was strolling past the jewelry store when he paused. Stuffing his hands into his jacket, Ryder went inside. His eyes slid past the rings and chains before settling on a Pandora set on display. Mesmerized, he moved toward the showcase.

When he saw what was inside up close, his breath caught. He circled the showcase several times. Each time, he grew more convinced that this was it. Every charm had different representations of what you might find in a garden—a rabbit, a watering can, lilies, a mushroom.

The saleslady came next to him. "This is the Pandora garden collection, meant to honor the beauty found in nature. Do you want to take closer look? It's the only one I have left and there have been many admirers but no takers so far."

"Can I?" he asked.

She used her tiny key to open the door and handed the piece to Ryder for closer inspection.

"This is perfect," he breathed out, then asked for the price. When she named the number, he let out a little whistle. But the more he held it, the more he loved it.

"You can get just the bracelet and one charm," she advised. "A lot of people do that and then add to it every year."

Squaring his shoulders, he shook his head. "I'll take the complete set. The woman I'm getting this for deserves the best."

"Look at the twinkle in your eyes. Your face is like a light bulb," the woman said, giggling. He stiffened, not liking the comparison. She went around the counter to ring up his order and then gift wrapped it.

Just then, Cara sent a text. Did you get your ugly sweater?

Yes. I have one with the Grinch and Gabby has one with princesses.

Let the contest begin. Wolf will decide on the winner.

No fair. You know he's going to choose you.

All's fair in a sweater war. She sent a heart emoji.

The saleslady must have been watching him, because she *tsk*ed. "I'd guess you were just texting your lady friend. Because you look besotted." Cocking her head, she said, "Love looks good on you."

Her words punched his gut. Whew. This was love. He was completely, madly, unequivocally in love with Cara. Suddenly, his chest lightened, and he couldn't hold back the wide grin. Why didn't anybody tell him that falling in love could feel so great? With sure steps, he approached the saleslady, handing her his card. "You're right. I am in love, and I can't wait to let her know it."

When he left, he found himself whistling a Christmas tune. For once, he was looking forward to the holiday—not just for Gabby but for himself. Ryder wanted to knock on Cara's door and holler out his feelings. But he would wait for Christmas. It would be the perfect day to offer her the most perfect gift of all—his love.

Chanel placed her gift for her sister under the small tree on her mantel, uttering a prayer for her safety. She hadn't decorated inside her home, partaking in all the Christmas activities with the Frosts instead. She packed her presents for Gabby, Wolf and Ryder in a large gift bag and adjusted her Christmas sweater.

Her red sweater sported a snowman and bells, and she'd paired it with black corduroy pants and boots. The air outside felt crisp, and temperatures were expected to drop low enough that Delaware might actually see snow on December twenty-fifth. Chanel couldn't remember the last time this state had had a white Christmas.

This evening, they were going to build the gingerbread house, and she was looking forward to stringing the popcorn on the tree. Gabby had been talking about that nonstop for the past few days. She zipped up her black coat and sailed through the front door. Then her eyes narrowed.

There was a black SUV coming down the road and making its way toward her driveway. Thinking it might be someone who was lost, she waited on the porch, expecting a window to roll down and the driver to ask for directions. Instead, the driver pulled right next to her pickup. Her stomach tensed, knowing who could be inside.

The passenger door opened and her sister stepped out, dressed in all black.

Dropping the packages, Chanel squealed and scampered down the steps to throw herself into her twin's arms.

"Cara!" she exclaimed before kissing her sister on both cheeks and then squeezing her tight again. "I can't believe it. You're back. I know you said you'd be back, but still. You're here."

"I didn't come back to get suffocated," Cara said, her voice muffled.

Chanel released her slightly, her eyes tearing up. "I'm so glad you're safe. Did you catch him?"

With tears in her eyes, Cara gave a nod. "It wasn't easy, but Jeremiah Greene is in custody and can't hurt anyone anymore."

She looked down at her sister's right leg. "How is your injury coming along?"

"I'm good," Cara said, pulling away. "Don't go making a fuss." She stuck her hands in her pockets and asked, "Where's my car?"

Giving her a light shove, Chanel chuckled. "I need to be asking you the same thing."

They looked at each other and said in unison, "Long story." Then, after a beat, said again in unison, "We'll talk later." This wasn't unusual for them to do, so they shrugged it off.

Cara grabbed Chanel's hand and walked her to the

driver's side. "We have so much to catch up on. Were you going somewhere?"

"Yes, I—"

Before Chanel could finish her sentence, a tall dark-skinned man with a slash across his right eyebrow, dressed in all black stepped out of the SUV. Chanel deduced he must be the FBI agent.

"Chanel, this is Agent Memphis Gray." Her sister blushed—actually blushed.

Memphis? Probably his undercover name. Cara must have read her mind, because she said, "And yes, it's his real name." Then she giggled, practically batting her eyes at the agent.

Looking between them, Chanel's eyebrows rose. She gave her sister's hand a double squeeze. Code that Chanel was going to get all the details later. Her sister sounded sappy and smitten. Cara squeezed back.

Memphis held out a hand. His voice was bass deep and butter smooth. "Pleased to meet you."

He had a firm handshake. Something Chanel appreciated.

Just then, a voice said, "Cara?" and Ryder came into view. He was holding Gabby's hand. Both had their coats open, so she could see they had on their ugly sweaters. Chanel froze and her mouth popped open.

In the excitement of her sister's return, she had forgotten Ryder had been expecting her. Of course he would come and check to see if she was okay. She watched as Ryder looked at her and her sister standing side by side. His brows knit in confusion before he gave a lopsided grin and his eyes settled on her.

He could tell them apart.

"Ms. Cara," Gabby boomed out. "There are two of you."

"Yes, yes, honey," she said, though she struggled to breath. "We're twins." This wasn't the way she envisioned Ryder finding out.

"Twins!" Gabby yelled, skipping over. "I love twins."

"Cara, you've been holding out on me," Ryder said, walking over, his eyes pinned on her. "Why didn't you tell me you were a twin? All these weeks, you never once said."

"Actually, *I'm* Cara," her sister interjected, her voice firm as she jabbed a finger to her chest. Then she pointed at Chanel. "This is my twin sister, Chanel." Then she smirked. "Hello, neighbor."

Ryder shook his head. "No. But…" His eyes darted between them several times, his confusion evident.

Gabby's brows furrowed, her little head turning back and forth between them. Chanel stooped until she was eye level with the little girl. Cupping Gabby's face, she said, "My real name is Chanel Houston." She gestured to her twin. "And that's my sister, Cara."

"Oh." Gabby put a hand to her mouth. "So you're not you?"

"No, I'm me. I just have a different name."

"But you lied, and Daddy said lying isn't good. Daddy said I shouldn't lie and say I brushed my teeth if I didn't!"

Cara snorted and Chanel cut her a warning glance. She held on to Gabby's shoulders. "Your daddy is right, and I'm sorry I wasn't honest. I was pretending to be my sister."

Gabby's eyes filled with sadness, which made Chanel's heart ache. "Did you pretend to play with me?" She returned to grab her father's hand—a sure sign that she was overwhelmed.

Ryder grunted and held his hand up. "Please stop speaking. You're only making things worse."

Chanel nodded and stood back, respecting his wishes. He held Gabby closer to him, his manner protective. She blinked to keep her tears at bay.

At this point, Memphis still hadn't uttered a word. He just rested against the SUV, his arms folded, watching the scene before him. Shaky, Chanel entreated her sister, "Cara, I'm sure you two must be exhausted from your drive. Why don't you go on inside and I'll catch up with you in a minute?"

Cara looked like she was about to argue. Then she heard a bark. Her face twisted. "Keep that flea-filled mutt away from me. I don't need him jumping on me and shedding his hairs all over my boots."

Cara's hate for Ryder's dog was all over her face.

"Let's head inside," Memphis suggested. He must have recognized that Cara had been about to go into confrontation mode. Chanel gave him a look of gratitude, amazed at how docile her sister became. Cara picked up the gift bag holding Chanel's gifts for the Frosts and took it inside the house.

The screen door slammed behind them.

Ryder bent over to whisper in Gabby's ear, and she gave a little nod. "Bye, Ms… I forgot your name."

Her chest tightened at that confession. "It's Chanel. You'll get used to it."

"Go back inside, sweetie," Ryder said gently. "I'll be in to start on our gingerbread house."

Gabby gave another little nod before signaling for Wolf to come with her. Chanel watched her departure, hating seeing the normally animated girl so quiet.

As soon as his daughter was out of earshot, Ryder

pounced. "Care to explain why you lied about your identity?" A muscle in his jaw twitched.

Wringing her hands, Chanel said, "My sister needed me to switch places while she hunted for Jeremiah Greene."

His eyes went wide. "So she didn't resign?"

"No. Cara had to go undercover to help the FBI track Jeremiah's whereabouts, and she couldn't risk any of his family alerting him."

"That's understandable."

She took a step forward. "I was going to tell you."

"When, exactly?" he asked, his tone cooler than the night temp.

"Tonight."

His brows knitted. "I can understand why you didn't say anything at first—but once we were friends, why didn't you confide in me and tell me the truth?"

She lifted her chin. "I gave Cara my word."

Ryder shook his head. "The thing is, I knew it. I knew something was off about you. There were tiny little clues that I chose to ignore. Well, actually, *huge* clues. Your entire personality was completely different. I should have asked questions."

"I—"

He cut her off, his chest heaving. "But I wouldn't have guessed in a million years that you switched places with your twin. No one in town ever mentioned Cara had a twin." His voice rose along with his fury. "Forget the town. *You* should have told me."

"I—I should have," she said, her lips quivering. "I haven't been here in years, and most of the people might not know about Cara being a twin. But I couldn't tell you. I had to protect my sister." She searched for more words, but her brain wouldn't cooperate. It was too busy keeping her blood pumping because her heart was breaking seeing Ryder's hurt and anger and knowing she was responsible.

"At my expense?" he yelled in frustration. "Cara, I…" His lips curled as he self-corrected. "Excuse me, *Chanel*." He repeated her name, testing it out on his tongue. "Chanel, I confided in you about things I've never told anyone. You should have trusted me to do the same. I'm not just anyone. Wait…am I?"

"Of course not," she pleaded, putting less space between them. "You must know what you mean to me." The urge to touch him was strong. She curled her fists, knowing that wouldn't be welcomed.

He scoffed. "How do I know that for sure? You were playing a role." His eyes turned fiery. "I was a fool. A fool to believe you."

"I'm still me," she said.

"Who you are? How can I know you when I don't even know your name? I don't know what was real and what was pretense," he snarled, pacing like a caged panther. "I can't believe this was all a prank between sisters."

She fought to get him to listen. "Nothing that happened between us was a pretense or a prank. I get that you're upset now, but when you've calmed down and had time to think about it, you'll realize that I genuinely care about you and Gabby."

He swung around to face her. "Don't utter my daughter's name. Gabby's mother has already disappointed her enough. I had to explain why Brittany isn't coming for New Year's like she planned and won't even be here for her surgery. But having you in her life removed that harsh sting. She talks about you and all the Christmas plans you made with her nonstop. And now Gabby doesn't even know your name." Anguish filled his face. "Do you know what that's like for her right now?"

"I—I didn't mean to hurt her. Or you."

"But you did. You hurt my little girl." His eyes glistened. "Stay away from us." He turned and stomped across her yard, heading over to his.

"She's expecting me to come help build the gingerbread house. I can't disappoint her," Chanel yelled out. "We said we'd make this Christmas special for her. Don't do this, please." Her shoulders shook.

Ryder swung around. "Gabby will be just fine without you. Don't kid yourself into thinking your deception will ruin our Christmas. I'll make sure that doesn't happen. So if you ever meant either of us any good, leave us alone. Neither my daughter nor I want or need an imposter in our lives."

Chapter Twenty-One

The stocking bearing the letters C-A-R-A mocked him. Ryder longed to snatch it and throw it into the fireplace, but knowing Gabby would ask questions made him refrain. When he had entered his house, Ryder had plastered a smile on his face and shouted, "Let the pre-Christmas celebrations begin!"

Gabby—who was sitting by the tree, moping—whooped for joy. "Yay! Is Ms. Cha—What's-Her-Name coming?"

"It's Chanel. And no, it's just me and you," he said, inserting enough enthusiasm to get his daughter excited. It would be just the two of them moving forward. With the help of YouTube, heated marshmallows and a triple dose of patience, Ryder and Gabby made their gingerbread house.

He took at least a hundred pictures, grateful for the opportunity to hide his face behind his cell phone to avoid his pain. His strategy was to stay busy all night long and not dwell on the fact that Cara—er, Chanel—wouldn't be there to celebrate his first Christmas in thirty-four years with him. It made him a little sad and a lot angry.

Ryder worked out some of his fury by chopping wood in his backyard for the fireplace. He wished he could howl like Wolf did with every chop, but he didn't want to scare Gabby.

Once he had a toasty fire going, he and Gabby roasted the marshmallows left over from building the gingerbread house. He was one marshmallow short of an upset stomach, but seeing Gabby's eyes shine was well worth it.

She squatted beside him as he sat by the tree, her face and hands sticky. "Look, Daddy, I'm going to be like Wolf." She licked her fingers.

"No, don't do that," he said. "Go wash your hands instead. Then come open one of your gifts."

Gabby complied without a fuss. Watching her skate across the floor in her socks made his heart warm.

"Which one do I open?" she asked, picking up a box and shaking it with vigor.

"Any you choose. Just check to see if it has your name."

He hid his grin because all the presents were hers. Some were for *Gabby, Gabrielle, Sweetie, Honey* and other nicknames. That had been Car—Chanel's suggestion. Ugh. It was going to take a minute to get used to that name. Not that he needed to, since she wouldn't be involved in their lives anymore. There he went thinking about her again.

Grabbing a box, he handed it to Gabby. "This is from your mother."

His daughter carefully undid the gift wrap. Chanel had wrapped this one. He gritted his teeth. She was everywhere. Well, at least he had gotten her name right this time.

"It's a doll," Gabby said with delight, twirling it in

different directions. The doll was dressed like an Egyptian queen. "It's beautiful. Ooh. I can't wait to see what else I got."

"Tomorrow." Ryder shot to his feet. "Let's make the popcorn so we can string the tree."

"Yippee," Gabby said, both her and her doll doing a jig. "How much do we need to make? Can I help? Are we going to use butter?"

"Slow down, little girl," he said, ruffling her hair. "We will probably have to make several bowls. Just promise you won't eat it all."

Lifting her right hand, she said, "I promise."

"Maybe I'll let you have some." He reached onto the shelf in the pantry to get the popcorn maker, the kernels and the butter-flavored oil.

"Yay. I can't wait to show Ms. Ca—that girl—my new doll."

Ryder placed his items on the counter and stooped to face her. "Honey, Ms. Chanel isn't coming tomorrow."

"Why isn't she coming?" Gabby's eyes filled. "Didn't she say that she was sorry? When I say I'm sorry, you say, no worries. Why can't you say that for Ms. Car—um, I mean Ms. Chanel?"

"It's not that simple, honey," he said. "Let's get back to what we're doing, okay?"

"Okay…" she mumbled.

Ryder seethed. Chanel had charmed her way into both their hearts. And now she was out, and he was left with so many questions. So many questions. But though Ryder could stop her from interfering in their lives, he couldn't expunge her from their hearts and thoughts that easily. Gabby might eventually forget, but for him, traces of her would echo for a long time. Maybe even for the rest of his life.

* * *

"Coming home for Christmas is supposed to be as sappy as the ending of a Hallmark movie," Cara said, holding Chanel close. They sat huddled together on her couch. Tissues had been tossed on the couch, on the coffee table and on the floor.

Memphis had long since retired to the guest room. Chanel suspected his ears had needed a break from her wailing.

"I am glad you're here," Chanel said, lifting her head. She knew her breath probably smelled of the pint of ice cream she had finished. Memphis had made a quick dash to the store, on Cara's orders, to grab a couple pints.

"Even though I ruined your evening with the Frosts?"

She could hear the regret in her sister's tone and shook her head. "You didn't. I should have told him."

"He's being an oversized infant," Cara said. "As a man of science, he should understand your rationale."

Chanel shook her head. "You don't get it. After all he's been through, this was the worst thing I could have done." Her shoulders shook. "Especially on Christmas Eve. Every time I close my eyes—" she hiccuped "—I see Gabby's face. I bet she's asking for me and wondering why I'm not over there." She laid her head on her sister's chest and sobbed.

"That Neanderthal is only thinking about himself," Cara fumed, her chest heaving hard. "As a father, he should consider Gabby's feelings."

"He's actually a good father." Chanel sniffled.

"Listen, if you're going to keep defending him, then how am I supposed to keep dogging him on your behalf?"

"I don't need you to degrade him…"

"Then what do you need?"

All Chanel could do was shrug. Her cell phone rang and she rushed to answer, hopeful that it was Ryder calling. She frowned. It was her old boss, Suzanne.

"I know I said to wait until after Christmas, but I need to know if you've made your decision. I gave my two weeks' notice, and I heard they might have another candidate in mind. So I want to add your name to the list."

Chanel bit her lip. She couldn't stay here, see Ryder next door and not be able to talk to him.

She glanced at her sister. Somehow in the midst of her tears about Ryder and Gabby, Chanel had managed to tell Cara about Suzanne's job recommendation. Cara gestured for her to think about it, but Chanel squared her shoulders. "If the board agrees, I'll take it."

"Great," Suzanne said. "You've earned it. Congratulations, and I'll be in touch."

Pressing the button to end the call, Chanel met Cara's scowling face. "I can't believe you're running again."

Chanel's mouth popped open. She looked at her twin's similar features like she had never seen them before. "Running?"

"Yes. You ran from this house, a place you loved, when Warren and your unborn child passed. You ran from me, our parents, leaving us to cope with the devastation of losing them and then you. You never came home for Thanksgiving or Christmas. Always making up some poor excuse—you're tired, you got lost, you had a deadline. It was so tiring that after a while, we stopped asking, expecting. And it was always up to me to visit you."

Cara licked her lips. "I thought after our parents died,

you would have come home. But you left me here alone to deal with this house and the memories by myself."

Chanel sat back, touching her chest. "I—I didn't know you saw things that way. I sound selfish."

"I wouldn't say that," Cara said, "More like, into yourself. You were so busy grieving that you didn't give us a chance to grieve with you."

"But this is different. Ryder is very much alive."

"No, it isn't different," she insisted. "You're in love with him, just as you were with Warren. And now all I can think is that it will be decades before you get over this one."

Chanel gasped. "I'm not in love."

"Yes. You are. It's plain to see." She splayed her hands. "You used an entire box of tissues and ate a pint of ice cream. That's not somebody who's mourning a friend-ship. That intense, drawn-out feeling of despair must be love. Can't be nothing else."

Releasing a long breath, Chanel said, "It crept up on me." Even she could hear the wonder in her tone. Fresh tears sprang to her eyes. After all this time, she loved a man who now despised her.

"What are you going to do?" Cara asked gently. "I know I would be over there knocking on his door, in-sisting he listen to me. That's what I would do."

"But I'm not you. I've got to do what feels right for me. I'm going back home to Virginia."

Chapter Twenty-Two

The banging on the door was too loud to ignore. Ryder raced down the stairs. It was almost 11:00 p.m. He had just convinced Gabby to go to bed, though she wasn't asleep. Who on earth would be at his house this time of night?

"Open the door, you idiot." It was a voice he recognized.

He swung the door open and turned on the porch light. "Chanel, I told you to—" He stopped and squinted. "You're not Chanel. Cara, what are doing here?" He could feel the cold seeping through his pajamas.

"You can tell us apart?"

"Yes. Of course. Chanel makes my heart smile. You…" He pointed. "You just make my head hurt."

His neighbor rolled her eyes, stuffed her hands into her jacket and pushed past him to get inside.

"Come in, why don't you?" With a sigh, he closed the door behind him.

Cara paused, looking around. There was wrapping paper on the floor, left there from when Gabby had opened a few more presents before going to bed. "Nice."

Wolf trotted in and the other woman seized up, fear

in her eyes. Ryder commanded Wolf to return to his spot. "What do you want?" he asked Cara, rubbing his temples.

"Besides telling you that you're a buffoon for hurting my sister?" she said. Eyes similar to Chanel's zoned in on him.

"Get to why you're here, please."

She stomped up to him and yelled, "Because of you, my sister is leaving for good."

His heart pierced. Chanel couldn't be leaving. "Wh-where is she going?" he sputtered.

"Back to Virginia, unless you have the good sense to stop her, Mr. PhD." She looked at her watch. "Chanel has a chance to get her dream librarian job and insists on leaving tonight, so if you're going to do something, now is the time."

Panic built like a crescendo. Ryder knew he couldn't let that happen. "Can you stay here with Gabby?" he asked.

"Take the dog with you," Cara said.

"He won't move." He dashed to the closet to get his coat, stuffed his feet into his boots and then was out the door.

He could see that Chanel was loading the pickup with boxes, so he made himself go faster.

Ryder jumped the stairs and dashed across the lawn. He didn't see the bucket of water and tripped over it, landing hard on the soil. His boot came off, and he was covered in dirt. Ryder hobbled home, only to see Cara standing on the porch, hollering and laughing.

"You look like a sorry-looking Cinder-fella reject," she snorted.

"Quit it!" he screamed. Then a little head popped out from behind Cara.

She was wiping her eyes. "Daddy, you look like a piggy rolling in the dirt."

This made Cara laugh even louder, raising her hand to high-five Gabby.

"Where are you going?" Gabby asked. Wolf rushed past Cara and came out to the porch, barking.

Cara jumped inside and slammed the screen door, staying on the other side of Wolf. "I thought you said he wouldn't move."

"I'm going to tell Ms. Chanel not to leave," Ryder said to Gabby.

"Can I come?" Gabby asked, her eyes earnest. "I want her to stay."

"Go get your coat," Ryder said, his heart pumping in his chest. Might as well make this a family affair.

Cara stepped outside. "This I gotta see."

Wolf ran to his side. Once Gabby returned, he began his second sprint across the yard. He could see the lights on in the truck.

"Chanel! Chanel!" he called out. Wolf barked and Gabby yelled her name as well.

Chanel paused with the last box of books in her hands. Her sister had given her the vehicle after explaining that her Chevy had met its demise in a ditch. Chanel knew better than to ask any more questions. She watched the sorriest procession she had ever seen crossing the lawn. Ryder led the pack, covered with dirt, Wolf was next and Gabby was behind. She squinted. Was that her sister taking up the rear?

Ryder raced over to her. Dirt was in his hair, on his face, all over his clothes. She had never seen him look so unkempt…or adorable. Thankfully, Gabby and Wolf looked fine.

"Chanel, your sister said you're leaving," he said. "Don't take that job, please."

"What does it matter to you what I do?" she asked, carting her box to the pickup. "You made it pretty clear that you didn't want me in your life."

Memphis came outside and leaned against the door-jamb. Cara led Gabby inside the house, then returned to stand by Memphis. Wolf went to sit by Memphis's feet causing her sister to put some distance between herself and the dog. Chanel closed the latch to the pickup and walked around to the driver's side.

"Chanel, please don't abandon us," Ryder said, trailing behind her, his voice cracking.

She gasped at his choice of words. "That's not fair, and you know it."

Ryder walked up to her and took her hand. "This isn't the way I planned to tell you—but, Chanel, you mean a lot to me. You have brightened my dull existence, and I need a lifetime to explain your significance in my life. We're peas and carrots."

Chanel paused for a moment, staring down at her hand in his. She looked up into his eyes. "An unlikely combination," Chanel said, tears falling down her face.

Dropping her hand, Ryder's eyes went wide. "Hold that thought." Then he took off, heading back to his house.

What just happened? Chanel wondered, shaking her head.

"I was wrong. Run, sis, run. Run while you can," Cara called out, shaking her head. "Because I don't know what's wrong with that man."

"Leave it alone," Memphis said.

A few minutes later, Ryder was back, sweating, his chest heaving although it looked like he had taken time

to wash his face and hands. "I have something for you."
He held out a square gift-wrapped box.

Her heart thundered. "Ryder, I don't know if... We
have a lot to talk about."

"Just open it," he nudged. "It will be all right."

She tore off the wrapper and opened the box. Her
breath caught. She lifted out the Pandora bracelet,
studying each charm. "Oh, it's beautiful." She touched
her chest. "Thank you so much."

"The other day, I went searching for a perfect gift.
Something that would show you what was in my heart."
He touched her face. His hand smelled like soap. "When
I found this bracelet, I thought to myself, it's perfect."
Stepping closer he said, "Then I realized that I loved
you with an intensity that scared but exhilarated me,
and I said, *that's* the perfect present. My love."

She sucked in her breath. "Oh, Ryder, I love you
too. I was too caught up in the past to realize it, but
you complete me."

"Hang on," he said, placing a finger over her lips.
"Though my love is the perfect gift, I knew it wasn't
enough."

"What else is there?" Cara asked.

Chanel's thoughts mirrored her sister's. She was
pretty sure she heard Memphis hush Cara, but she con-
centrated on the man before her.

"My love, if you'll have me, I'd like to offer you the
ultimate gift of all—my family. Gabby, Wolf and I are
a package deal, and we would love for you to join us.
For always."

This time her heart melted, and Chanel snatched him
close. "You really have a way with words. Yes, yes, I'll
have you all. For life," she choked out before crushing

her lips to his. They shared a long, deep passionate kiss before breaking apart.

Chanel could have sworn she heard her sister say, "You redeemed yourself."

"To be continued…" Ryder promised, reaching up to cup her head, his fingers running across her hearing aid. His brows furrowed and he lifted her hair to take a peek. His eyes went wide.

She cracked a smile. "I told you we had plenty to talk about. It might take a lifetime before you learn all you need to know."

Drawing her close, he declared, "A lifetime with you will never be enough."

Chanel wrapped her arms around him, knowing she was finally home. For good.

Epilogue

The following year...

It was snowing in Delaware!

On Christmas Day. Chanel stood by the window early in the morning, sipping her hot cocoa and admiring the silent, falling snow. Wolf sat close to her feet, and she was careful not to step on him.

A strong pair of arms encircled her from behind and drew her close before lips brushed her ear.

She smiled and lifted a hand to touch Ryder's head. "Merry Christmas, sleepyhead."

"Sleepyhead? It's only a little after six."

Chanel turned to face her husband of three months. "I've been up for about an hour, putting the gifts under the tree." They walked toward the huge evergreen in the corner of the room, which was covered in stringed popcorn, sparkling lights and homemade ornaments.

His eyes shone. "I can't wait to see Gabby's face when she spots the new bike we bought her."

"I think she's going to be more excited about the books than the bike, but we'll see." Gabby loved to read and had graduated from picture books to chapter books.

She and Chanel had persuaded Ryder to have an extra-long bench swing on their porch. When the weather permitted, they would huddle together and read.

Ryder took her hand and led her to sit on the couch before going to the tree to get a small box. Chanel eyed his pajamas featuring trees and snowman before smoothing the pants of her matching pj's. It looked like he had a small handprint on the back of his shirt. Her lips quirked. She bet it was from the gingerbread house they had put together. Gabby's hands had been a mess, but she'd had a lot of fun.

Finding the package, Ryder returned to her side of the couch. "Mrs. Frost—I don't think I'll ever get tired of saying that—I'd like you to open this before Gabby gets up."

Her mouth dropped. "I thought we agreed that we weren't going to buy each other anything. What about us being each other's perfect gift?"

"I know. But I couldn't resist." He patted her hand. "Open it."

Chanel undid the wrapping paper, opened the box and gasped. It was a gold chain and locket ensconced in a satin cloth. Her eyes shot up to meet Ryder's. "It's beautiful." She picked up the delicate piece of jewelry and opened the locket. There was a picture of Gabby with her front teeth missing on one side and another of her and Ryder on their wedding day on the other. She dabbed at her eyes. "I love it. Thank you so much." Ryder placed it around her neck, and she cupped the locket with her hands. "I'll treasure it always."

They shared a tender kiss before Chanel broke free and stood. "Since we're exchanging presents…"

He lifted a brow. "So you broke the agreement as well?"

She nodded before going to get a flat box with his name on it. She had wrapped it with black wrapping paper and silver trimmings. While he opened the box, she couldn't keep the tears from falling down her cheeks. Her chin wobbled and her hands felt clammy.

"What's wrong?" he asked.

"Just open it," she whispered.

He picked up a small four-by-six photograph and squinted. "What's this?"

She smiled, her eyes wetting with tears. "Our son. As soon as I saw his little face, I knew. He was the one." Ryder and Chanel had decided to adopt another child while Gabby was young so she could have a playmate.

Ryder's scooped her in his arms and sprinkled kisses across her face. "What do you think Gabby will say?"

She touched his cheek and chuckled. "We'll find out soon enough."

A couple hours later, when Gabby heard the news, she squealed, "A new brother! Yay! I always wanted one of those."

* * * * *

If you enjoyed this story, don't miss
Zoey Marie Jackson's next emotional romance,
available next year from Love Inspired!

Find more great reads at www.LoveInspired.com.

Dear Reader,

I wrote Chanel and Ryder's story while going through the toughest time in my life. I found myself relating to these characters in a way I didn't expect. God used their path to healing and hope to minister to me and give me a strength I had no idea I possessed.

Chanel and Ryder each had painful memories from their pasts that served as a wedge to them moving forward. Watching them open their hearts to God's word and then each other gave me hope and lifted my spirits, especially when Chanel and Ryder found the perfect gift of all was each other and family. I am still waiting for my blessing and I wish you the same.

I love reading—and now writing—about twins. Especially twins who decide to switch roles. Doing this for adult twins was a bit tricky, but I think it gave this special story an enjoyable twist. I would love to hear your thoughts. Please connect with me on Facebook or join my newsletter at www.zoeymariejackson.com.

Zoey Marie Jackson

CHRISTMAS ON HIS DOORSTEP
North Country Amish • by Patricia Davids

To save her sister's puppy from their legal guardian's wrath, Jane Christner drops the dog off on the doorstep of neighbor Danny Coblentz. The Amish teacher is determined to help Jane and her sister find a better life in his community this Christmas. Could it also lead to love?

AN AMISH CHRISTMAS WISH
Secret Amish Babies • by Leigh Bale

Newly widowed, Seth Lehman needs help caring for his nine-month-old daughter. He offers Susanna Glick free use of his empty storefront for her noodle business if she'll also watch baby Miriam while he tends both their farms. But as Christmas draws closer, their arrangement begins to feel like a family...

AN ALASKAN CHRISTMAS PROMISE
K-9 Companions • by Belle Calhoune

Kit O'Malley is losing her sight and begs local rancher Leo Duggan to let her have one of the service puppies he is training. As they work together, the single mom gains hope of a more normal life, but there's a secret that could tear them apart...

A CHRISTMAS BARGAIN
Hope Crossing • by Mindy Obenhaus

When single mom Annalise Grant inherits a Texas Christmas tree farm and discovers a portion of her trees are on her neighbor's property, she'll do anything to hold on to them—including suggesting a collaboration with the handsome rancher next door. Will a compromise turn into the family neither expected?

HER CHRISTMAS REDEMPTION
by Toni Shiloh

After a past riddled with mistakes, Vivian Dupre needs a second chance in her new town—and helping with the church's Christmas Wishes program is the best place to start. But as she and Michael Wood work to fulfill wishes, can Vivian keep her secrets from thwarting her own holiday dreams?

A SECRET CHRISTMAS FAMILY
Second Chance Blessings • by Jenna Mindel

Ruth Miller and Bo Harris enter a modern-day—and secret—marriage of convenience to save Ruth's home as well as her late husband's business. Despite their intention to keep the relationship strictly business, love starts to bloom. But the truth about Ruth's first husband might shatter their fragile marriage deal forever.

LICNM1022

HARLEQUIN
PLUS

Announcing a **BRAND-NEW** multimedia subscription service for romance fans like you!

Read, Watch and Play.

Experience the easiest way to get the romance content you crave.

Start your **FREE 7 DAY TRIAL** at
<u>www.harlequinplus.com/freetrial</u>.